THE LEGEND CONTINUES

Doc Holliday called him "the fastest gun I ever saw . . ." He was Buckskin Frank Leslie: gambler, sportsman, pimp, and mad-dog killer—until the girl he loved was shot down in a gunfight that he had provoked.

That same night, Buckskin Frank Leslie—friend to Holliday and the Earps, sworn enemy of the Texan gunmen, Ben Thompson and Clay Allison—left town. Rode out—and was never heard of again.

Never heard of—except for odd rumours . . . legends . . .

—About a man named "Fred Lee," who tried to settle down on a ranch in Montana—only to blaze a bloody trail through the valley of the Rifle River. . . and ride away.

—And about a man named "Farris Lea . . ."

BUCKSKIN #2

GUNSTOCK

Roy LeBeau

LEISURE BOOKS ✿ **NEW YORK CITY**

To the Macdougal Street gang

A LEISURE BOOK

Published by

Dorchester Publishing Co., Inc.
6 East 39th Street
New York City

Printed in the United States of America

CHAPTER ONE

Farris Lea had been waiting for an elk for two hours.

Lea was a tall, lean man, his clean-shaven face burned deep mahogany by the mountain sun. His dark hair was flecked with gray at the temples, the same shade of gray as his deep-set eyes. He was sitting high on the slope of Edge mountain—named, not for its saw-spined ridge, but for a trapper, Ephriam Edge, who'd hunted the Bitteroots half a century before.

The elk was past due. Lea had sent Tocsen scouting past the mountain shoulder to spook the bull elk down the draw and into the broad, autumn-brown meadow below.

There, with any luck at all, his Lordship, Baron the Graff Rudiger von Ulm-und-Felsbach would manage to shoot the damn thing.

Lea shifted the heavy Sharps across his lap. He shouldn't need it for backup on the elk; not this time anyway. The Baron was a squarehead pain in the ass, but he could shoot. The Sharps was for grizzly.

The big bears were thick in the Bitteroots now, just

before the snow came in for good. Old Abe Bridge had warned Lea about them when he'd hired him on as hunting guide. "Just two years ago, I lost a fat French banker to one of those pig-bears! And I don't damn well intend to lose another paying guest in that fashion! Understand me, Lea?"

Lea understood him. Old Abe Bridge was the sole owner and proprietor of the biggest, finest, fanciest, and most expensive resort hotel in the west. Gunstock was a luxury resort, for sure, but it wasn't set up in some civilized place like Denver or the north of California.

Gunstock, all 600 rooms, was stuck way out in the lonesome, deep in Idaho's Bitteroot mountains. The rich dudes who came by train and stagecoach from the East expected to get the Wild West served up to them on a plate. And Farris Lea, the Shoshones, and the grizzlies were expected to oblige.

Gunstock was Abe's pride and joy, a million-dollar dream that had taken every penny of the old prospector's one big lucky strike: a fortune in silver dug out of the old grubstake in Colorado.

Abe had hired Lea on almost a year before, when he'd come riding his big dun through the mountains, heading for the Pacific coast, dead broke. It happened that Abe's previous guide, a handsome halfbreed named Dark Cloud, who'd been a great favorite with the lady guests, had wound up under a pack mule after a thousand-foot fall.

Abe had noticed Lea out behind the kitchens, cutting some firewood to pay for his supper, had stopped to talk, and must have found something about Lea that he liked. He'd offered him the job on the spot, and a plum

6

job it was, if you enjoyed kissing the butts of robber barons, politicians, and the odd European nobleman out for a backwoods time.

Well, Lea hadn't enjoyed the butt-kissing and had refused to do it. He'd held onto the job anyway. The guests had enjoyed his independent air and sometimes Lea even enjoyed the hunting. And if, as it happened, he had spent some time in Chicago, and more time than that on the rougher fringes of San Francisco society, there was no need for the dudes to know that. They were happier thinking their guide was a right mountain man who wouldn't know the proper way to order a beer in a barrel house.

Well, that was fine with Lea. He'd caught on quick to the theatrical part of the job, and he acted the frontiersman like Bill Cody himself. It was a good job, all in all, and old Abe still liked him, even if his daughter didn't. Blue-eyed Sarah had cold-shouldered Lea from the start, thinking he was just some smooth-tongued drifter taking advantage of Abe. And it seemed she thought his predecessor, Dark Cloud, to have been the perfect noble savage, and Farris Lea a pretty poor substitute.

Lea had kept out of her way as much as he could, and kept doing his job as well as he could. He had not bothered to tell Sarah Bridge what old Tocsen had told him, namely, that Dark Cloud's real Blackfoot name had been "He-That-Farted," and that the halfbreed had gone in terror of the Shoshones who roamed the Bitteroots.

The Shoshones hadn't bothered Lea yet, or Gunstock. Abe had had the smarts to talk to their peace-chief, a man called Side-of-the-Hill, and had arranged some payments of food, horses, and blankets. Gunstock was a visiting place for the whites, not a settling place. And as long as that was true, and the Army kept a garrison at Salt River, the Shoshones would stay peaceable. Lea had seen them many times, shadowing his hunting party along the ridges, and the dudes had been thrilled—and a little scared—when he'd pointed them out. But the Indians never came closer.

Tocsen was a Shoshone, of what rank Lea had never found out, though his clan was Turtle, and that was maybe another reason the Shoshone didn't come in for trouble.

The old Indian had just walked into one of Lea's camps one night, settled down by the fire without a word, eaten supper—while a New England ship owner sat staring, bug-eyed—and in the morning had simply gone to work, catching and packing up the horses, striking the camp tents, and boiling the breakfast coffee.

He'd been working with Lea ever since. And he was worth his weight in whatever Lea might have chosen to name. The old man had a nose for game to beat any buffalo hunter or trapper Lea had ever known, and, unlike many Indians, he was a damn good shot.

All in all, he had a good job. And in country as pretty as the country Lea had left. But there was no use thinking about that. No use at all.

He sat up suddenly, tightening his grip on the Sharps. Something had moved down in the breaks by the mouth of the draw. Nothing. Nothing, for maybe a full minute. The chill autumn wind swept across the frost-killed grass carpeting the meadow below. Lea hoped that the Baron hadn't gone to sleep on him. He'd seen more than one dude lose a shot for not being able to stay awake in a stand.

Then Lea saw it. A bull elk with a rack like a moose's slowly, slowly walking out of the brush into the open. Tocsen had done it just right, as usual. He'd moved the elk out, but hadn't spooked him. The square-headed Baron wouldn't get a finer shot at a finer animal in his life.

Lea rose to his feet in one easy motion, the barrel of the big rifle balanced across his left forearm. He shrugged off the long buffalo coat he'd draped across his shoulders, and stood alert, staring down into the valley below. He was wearing plain brown cowhide boots with low hill-country heels, dark-brown wool trousers, a wool plaid shirt, and a handsomely fringed buckskin vest, decorated with fine Indian beadwork. As the cold wind blew through the Bitteroots, the soft buckskin folded back momentarily in the breeze, and the long fringe fluttered against the worn walnut butt of a short-barreled Bisley Colt .45, worn high and forward on his right side, the butt slanting back to just above his hip.

Why the hell wasn't that German taking his shot? The elk was a hundred yards out into the meadow now. As Lea watched, it suddenly stopped, its great head lifted, swinging as it tested the air. And the same moment, Lea felt the mountain wind begin to shift direction, short gusts drafting along the mountainside, turning more and more from the north. The elk would be smelling sauerkraut in a few seconds: why didn't the son-of-a-bitch shoot?

Then came the shot. Lea froze, the butt of the Sharps halfway to his shoulder.

9

The big elk staggered as the brittle, echoing crack of the Mannlicher died away. The Baron had made his shot. And too damn high. As Lea watched, the bull elk recovered, stumbled, then sprang into a hard driving run toward the brush at the end of the valley. *No good,* Lea thought. *You made the wrong move, brother. You should have turned back to the draw.*

The elk was only yards from the border of the brush when the German's rifle spoke again. The big animal seemed to collapse all at once, like a huge puppet with cut strings. It fell, and rolled once, and was still. Lea sighed and lowered the hammer on the Sharps. The end of the hunt was always the saddest part.

He had taken only two steps down the mountainside when a third shot rang out, and he saw the animal jolt to the bullet's impact. The Baron apparantly liked to make sure that dead was dead. That was usually a pretty good idea. It had been Lea's idea, too, once upon a time.

"That first shot was not my fault!"

The Baron had never admitted that anything was his fault during the four days Lea had been guiding him.

"Let me see that rifle," Lea said. He'd never cared for the Baron's Mannlicher. It was a neat piece, and very finely made—a match piece, actually. That was just the trouble with it. It was not a weapon for rough handling in rough country, at least not in country as rough as the Bitteroots in November. It had jammed at the breech twice already in the last few days; and once had cost the Baron one of the handsomest mountain sheep that Lea had seen since he came to Gunstock.

The Baron handed it over with a grunt. They were standing beside the elk while Tocsen butchered it out. The old Shoshone had come trotting out of the draw on his little pinto just as Lea had walked down the mountain slope. "Nice driving, old man," Lea had said to him. "Yes," the old man had said, and nodded, "I push elk good." He'd swung off his pinto, drawn his knife, and gotten to work on the elk. Tocsen wasn't much for long speeches.

Lea looked the Mannlicher over carefully, keeping his ungloved hands off the beautifully polished steel. It was the sight for sure. The Baron had ridden out of the hotel stables with a fine telescopic sight on the rifle. The fine sight had lasted for two days, then a pack horse had walked over the rifle while they were striking camp by Turkey River. The sight had bent like licorice candy.

"You have a bent sight, Baron," Lea said. "The shot wasn't your fault. Matter of fact, you made a damn nice second shot there, considering." *That ought to hold the son-of-a-bitch,* Lea thought.

The Baron was a big man, with blank blue eyes and iron-gray hair, cropped close. He looked a little fat, but he wasn't; he was strong as a horse. If he'd had something of a sense of humor, and been willing to pitch in somewhat to help with the camp work—which a lot of the better dudes were happy to do—then he would have been a fair enough hunting partner. But the Baron had no sense of humor at all, and didn't appear to enjoy anything much except shooting, and he never, never lifted a finger in camp. Lea and Tocsen did all the doing, and that was that. It made for a stiff, unfriendly hunt.

"Can you fix dat?" the Baron said. He spoke English well, but he had a tough time with *th*.

"No," Lea said, "It would take a gunsmith and gunsmith's tools to get that sight-leaf straight." He punctuated that by spitting a little tobacco juice to the side.

11

The Baron muttered something in German. "What did you say?" Lea said.

"I said," said the Baron, "what de hell am I to shoot wit, now?" He looked considerably annoyed. None of the Gunstock guests liked to have anything go wrong. It seemed to make them nervous. And the Baron liked it less than most.

"You use the Martini-Henry," Lea said. The Martini was new, a nice weapon, well-balanced and easy to shoot, and it had the strongest action made. The rifle's only fault was the moderate striking power of its ammunition. You couldn't be sure of knocking a big animal down with the first shot. But that was what Lea and the Sharps were for.

The Baron made a face, and glared down at the Mannlicher as if it had personally insulted him. Lea decided to earn his money.

"It's a beautiful firearm, Baron, but it just wasn't made for these here conditions. And that's a fact." He spit a bit more tobacco juice. "I guess you Germans make about the *nicest* firearms there is." The Baron looked a little happier, and grunted.

"I will use de Martini," he said.

"You look," old Tocsen said. He was standing up beside the half-butchered elk. He'd already gutted it, and caped-out the head and rack for salting. The Baron liked to have something to show.

"Men come," the old Shoshone said. He was looking down the valley.

There were three men riding slowly down the valley toward them. They were still a good way off, and didn't seem to be in any hurry, ambling along—but coming on straight, just the same. It was the rifle shots that had fetched them, of course. The three of them, still a couple of hundred yards off, rode abreast down

12

the middle of the valley meadow, their horses stepping high through the cold, damp grass.

They didn't look good. They looked too easy, too relaxed at meeting three strangers in the middle of nowhere. Lawmen? Maybe. Lea didn't think so. There were too many of them for serving papers, too few for a posse. Besides, the Gunstock range was a long way from Boise—or from any other law-station, for that matter.

"Load that Mannlicher, Baron," Lea said. The German was somewhat familiar with trouble. He breeched a round into the Mannlicher and didn't say a word.

Lea looked around for Tocsen, but the old Shoshone wasn't there; he'd ghosted back up to the tree line. Lea saw him bend over a pack for a moment, then straighten with a double-barreled Greener in his hands —loaded with double-ought, and both hammers back.

The three men were coming in. The one riding in the middle was smiling in a friendly way. Lea reached down and eased the keeper-loop off the hammer of his Colt. If there was trouble, it was going to be trouble close-in.

"Howdy!" the middle one called. He was still smiling, a very friendly fellow.

None of the three looked like much, either for good or bad, but Lea didn't spend much time on that. Looks didn't mean much for a killer, or a good man either. The middle man was a thin fellow with a three-day beard and bright brown eyes. The man riding on his right was big and haunchy, with dirty blond hair done up in a couple of pigtails. He looked a bit like a squaw man. The third rider, off to the smiler's left, was a sallow-faced kid, maybe seventeen years old, maybe not. All of them were armed.

Lea saw this much in one fast glance, but it wasn't what interested him. What interested him was

13

the horses.

Their horses were dead beat. Wind-broke, spur-scarred, and worn. The three of them must have roweled the animals sharp to bring them down the meadow so lively—trying to cover their condition.

Whatever their reasons, whatever their trouble, these men needed fresh horses badly.

"Say now," the smiler said, "that's what a man could call a real prime elk you fellers got there."

The sallow boy wasn't paying attention to the talk. He was looking over to the nearby tree line. Looking at Tocsen and the Greener. Looking at the horses.

It was a prime string: Lea's big dun, the Baron's fancy bay stallion, Tocsen's little pinto, and three first-class Morgan-cross pack horses. Abe outfitted with nothing but the best. Nothing else would do for Gunstock.

The sallow boy was eating those animals up with his eyes.

"I guess you fellers couldn't spare say a quarter of that elk deer, now could you? We could sure do with some prime fixin's. We'll pay gold."

"Ain't that so, Louis?" the smiling man said, real sharp, to the sallow boy. He'd seen Lea notice that hungry look at the horses. The boy turned back slowly, not worried and not hurried.

"I suppose," he said. He wore a Smith & Wesson Russian model .44, fixed for a left-hand cross draw.

"We could use some meat for sure," the big pigtailed man said. He had a soft, pleasant voice, and colorless eyes.

"Who's the dude?" the smiling man said, looking at the Baron.

The Baron's meaty face flushed up turkey red. He wasn't used to people talking down to him like that. The smiling man saw the flush, and smiled wider. "No

14

offense," he said.

While he said it, the sallow boy kneed his horse a step or two farther out to the smiler's left, out to the side.

Lea had seen it all before, a lot more times than he cared to remember. He wasn't even angry at them.

"Listen to me," he said to the smiling man. "Listen carefully. If your bad-boy there moves his horse one more step to the side, or moves his left hand at all, the old Indian is going to kill him. Then, I'll kill you and pigtail."

The smiler heard him out, but his smile got a little stiff. Lea felt, rather than saw, the sallow boy shift in his saddle.

"You're about to get killed," he told the smiling man.

"Hold it!" the smiling man said to the boy. Then he stopped smiling and stared down at Lea.

"All right," he said, glancing down at Lea's holstered Colt, then back up to his face. "All right. We're not looking for shooting." He paused, looking into Lea's eyes. "But, I'll tell you, Mister, we need those horses. We *need* them, and that's flat!"

"We sure do," the pigtailed man said.

"Now," said the middle man, and he started smiling again, "we will pay you folks a real good price for those animals . . . in gold. And I mean a real good price."

"That's right," the pigtailed man said. The sallow boy said nothing.

"Now what do you say about that?" said the smiler.

Lea smiled back at him. "Turn and ride out of this camp," he said. "And keep riding. If you don't, we'll shoot your buttons off."

The smiling man stared down at Lea for almost a full minute.

"You folks are being unreasonable," he said quietly.

"Baron," Lea said, "when I kill this man, shoot the

15

big one with the pigtails.''

"I vill do dat," the Baron said. "I haf kilt men before dis time!"

The smiling man was no fool. Seeing cruelty, or courage, or savage temper in Lea's face wouldn't have impressed him at all. But he saw none of those things. He saw a man considering a familiar job of work, and nothing very speeial, at that. It was a look the smiling man had seen before.

Even so, he might have made a play. He had considerable confidence in the boy's draw. And in himself and Squaw Murrey, too.

Something else stopped him. He'd seen this hunter before, and he was damned if he could remember where. It had been a long time ago. Years ago. But he couldn't remember who, and he couldn't remember where.

The smiling man, who was a bank robber named Thomas Deke, decided to pick a better time.

"Well, hell," he said, and leaned in the saddle to spit, "if you people want to act so damn unfriendly, then to hell with you!" And he turned his horse's head. "Come on, boys," he said to his men, "we'll leave these assholes be."

CHAPTER TWO

His men looked surprised—especially the boy, and for a moment, Lea thought the kid was going to lose his temper and open the ball on his own; but the smiling man, not smiling now, flashed the boy a cold, hard glance, and the kid slowly turned his horse and followed after the other two.

Lea stood where he was and watched them go, not bothering to spur up their tired animals now, riding away at a walk. None of the three looked back.

"Should ve kill dem?"

"No," Lea said. "We don't kill them. Not now."

It looked for a minute as though the Baron was going to argue about it. He stared after the three riders, the Mannlicher balanced in his hands. His blank blue eyes weren't so blank now.

"If they come at us again, we'll fight," Lea said. "All they've done so far is give us hard looks and offer to buy our horses."

The Baron grunted and shook his head, unconvinced. He apparently was a bloodthirsty Baron back home.

They stuck camp, Tocsen finishing the butchering of the elk, and Lea striking the tents and packing the horses. The Baron, as usual, didn't do a damn thing. He sat on a folding camp stool, the Mannlicher across his lap, and looked out down the valley, probably hoping the three drifters would come galloping back full charge.

Tocsen finished with the elk, and lugged the quartered meat and salted trophy-head over to Ranger, the one pack horse that didn't mind the smell of blood. It took him three trips for the meat alone.

The old man helped Lea pack the meat into the diamond frames. Then they set the head and cape atop the load, and braced the gunny-sacked bundle with cross lashings. Gunstock guests were mighty particular about their trophies.

Tocsen said nothing about the three horse-hungry drifters; the subject didn't seem to interest him. When the men had ridden away, he'd just eased the hammers of the Greener, and then gone back to camp to unload it and put it away. Then he'd gotten back to his butchering.

"We'll go back by High Pass," Lea said to him, and the old man nodded and finished the lashings. High Pass was an awkward way to go. It would cost at least another day getting back to Gunstock, and it was a bad way for the horses, stony and narrow, above gullies and gorges. High Pass was the place where Dark Cloud had wound up a thousand feet down a mountain and under a mule. Lea had traversed it several times, once in a bad blizzard. It was no pleasure, but with a little care it

18

could be done. It was also a way the three drifters were unlikely to know.

"Baron, we're going back to the hotel a different way," Lea said, when they were mounted and ready to move. "It's a mountain pass I know; it shouldn't give us too much trouble this time of year."

"You do dis to avoid dos tree?" the Baron said, reining his big stallion in. That was a very testy horse, that bay. The Baron was settling down from the near fight, Lea noticed. He was pronouncing his *v's* just fine now. Only the *th's* were still giving him trouble.

"That's right," Lea said. "That's exactly the reason. I'm not paid to bring in dead guests, Herr Baron." The 'Herr Baron' should go down pretty well, Lea thought.

"I don't run from dogs like dat!" the Baron said, and he gave Lea a careful look. "It is not, is it, dat you are a coward, Mr. Lea?"

For an instant, Lea felt his temper rising, and just as quickly, he got it under control. This squarehead was used to riding people roughshod; he probably had no idea that Lea, a hired hand, might take serious offense. Why should he? For the Baron, and for people like him, real courage was the property of gentlemen, not backwoods roughnecks.

"No, Baron," Lea said, and forced a smile, "I'm no coward. And I'm not any damn fool, either." And he turned the dun's head to lead out of camp. The Baron's broad face was red as a turkey cock's as he spurred his stallion after.

Hours later, deep into afternon, they were climbing. Snaking back and forth up the steep ridge to the mountain Abe Bridge called Saddleback. And that mountain was only a first step up the long reach to

19

Collier's Hill and High Pass.

Lea turned in his saddle to see how the Baron and the pack string were making out. No problem with the Baron; the German was a good horseman, in a stiff, cavalry sort of way. He sat his big bay stallion like a statue in a park. He noticed Lea looking back at him, and immediately looked away, pretending to admire the scenery, which was something considerable to admire. The Baron was still annoyed over being called a damn fool. A hired hand had nipped at him, and he didn't like it.

Lea looked farther back, checking old Tocsen and the string. The old man was going fine, as always, singing to himself, rocking along on that fat little pinto. Lea wondered again why the old Indian had come in to work with him. Tocsen didn't seem to care for whites very much, and Lea was under no illusion that he was an exception to that. The old man got along with him, worked with him, put up with him—and that was about all.

The pack string was stepping along, taking the slope in stride, moving up. Three good solid horses. They had to be. By next morning they'd be pacing along trails not three feet wide, spiked thick with granite shards, and edging off into clear sky blue, empty, as far as a man could see.

Ranger, Button, and Candy Cane were loaded with pack saddles, blankets, bridles, halters, stake ropes, hobbles, lash ropes, panniers, pots and pans, tarps, tools, tents, and a big chuck box full of everything from canned peaches to horse liniment. Three fine and heavy-laden horses worth killing for.

* * *

They made the ridge of Saddleback before dark, and Lea called a halt there for the night. They pulled up in a long, level clearing just past a stand of aspen. Lea and Tocsen hobbled the horses, and staked them out to graze in the clearing. It was sparse, this late in the year, and frost-burned, but it would do the animals some good, and, with a feed-bag each of grain, would carry them to Collier's Hill the next day.

The Baron, still with nothing to say to Lea, took his folding canvas camp chair up to a little rise beyond the aspens, took a fine pair of field glasses out of their case, and sat scanning the countryside below—some thirty miles of mountainside, valleys, river-breaks and forest —for sign of the three drifters. Nothing wrong with that. It was just what Lea had had in mind himself.

He took the battered little telescope—it was battered because it had taken that long fall with Dark Cloud— out of his saddle bag, and walked over to join the Baron on his little rise. The Baron rolled an eye at him, but didn't say anything.

For a few minutes, they scanned the country below them.

Finally, the Baron stood up with a grunt, and put his fine field glasses back into their case.

"Dey are not dere," he said.

"Maybe," said Lea. "Maybe they aren't."

"Vit dose horses, dey don't keep up," said the Baron, and he went off the way he usually did at a halt, to find some tree cover and piss in private.

It was likely the Baron was right. They could, of course, have kept up by letting the boy, the lightest of them, take all three horses—leading two behind him— and ride them by turn as they tired. But that would mean leaving the other two men afoot. Not likely.

So, they couldn't follow. Lea had set a stiff pace throughout the afternoon. It had wearied their own fine mounts, and the pack horses as well. The three ragged mounts under the drifters wouldn't have been able to make half the miles in half the time.

Lea closed his eyes, trying to remember, to picture the drifters, their horses. The smiler and the boy had talked Texican. Some time away from it, maybe, but Texas voices all the same. Not pigtail, though. And their rigs? The boy had forked a Brazos double, a Texas saddle, Lea was sure enough of that; but try as he might, he couldn't be certain of the other men's rigs.

It came down to pigtail. If he knew the Bitteroots, he'd know that High Pass was the long way around, picked just to weary them off the track. And sure as hell, he'd lead his partners across the Pace River breaks and through the gap to Gunstock. If that was so, all three of them would be sitting at the other end of High Pass by tomorrow's sunset, waiting.

There wasn't much chance of that, but there was enough of a chance for Lea to worry about. The Baron might still be able to show him up for a damn fool after all.

It depended on pigtail.

Lea had learned long ago that enough worry was enough. If he'd called it wrong, he'd damn sure find it out at the other end of High Pass.

Lea walked over to the campfire. Tocsen had dug a pit first, and built the fire down in it to keep the flame from showing through the mountains.

Lea grubbed in the chuck box, and came out with the last can of peaches and the bottom siftings of flour.

He'd use elkfat for shortening. It made for a strong-tasting pie, but he'd fed it to some mighty picky eaters, used to Europe's best, and gotten no complaints. He and Tocsen had an unspoken agreement: Tocsen cooked the meat, and Lea did the fancy fixin's. Lea'd learned to bake the camp pies and breads in the gigantic kitchens at Gunstock, where, occasionally, the head chef, a very fat and temperamental Frenchman named de la Maine, had made a face of disgust and then given Lea a word of advice.

By the time Lea had his pie dough rolled out and tucked down into the greased Dutch-oven, Tocsen grunted and rattled the tines of the big meat fork on the light iron grill that Candy Cane had been hauling over the mountains for the last four days. It was the Shoshone's announcement that the steaks were ready.

There were three thick, long slabs of prime elk loin, rubbed with cracked black pepper and butter scooped from a Gunstock storehouse crock, and studded with slivers of the little wild onions that grew along the Bitteroot streams in late autumn. All three of them lay sizzling over a raked bed of dull red aspen coals. Tocsen forked one up and slapped it down in one of the big tin platters, scooped up more butter to smear on the smoking meat, and tossed a knife and bent fork onto the plate beside it.

It was rough service, and the old Shoshone never varied it, not for Grand Dukes, not even for railroad kings. But after tasting the old man's cooking, all the dudes seemed glad enough to put up with his lack of manners. The Baron was no exception. He'd been standing by the fire, waiting, and was eager to take that first steak, bent fork and all.

Lea was finishing the peach pie. He poured the canned fruit into the pastry shell, topped it with butter, folded the top edges of the pastry over for an upper crust, and then slid the covered Dutch-oven deep under a lifted shovelful of coals. Then he picked up his own steak, scraped a little salt over it from the salt cake in the chuck box, pulled his sheath knife, and cut his first, dripping, red-centered slice, almost two inches thick, and still cooking in its own sputtering juices.

The pie was ready by moonrise. Lea took his portion, walked down through the aspens, and stood munching the sugary-tart crustiness, watching the silvery moonlight slowly flood the land beneath him. It looked too beautiful to be dangerous.

CHAPTER THREE

They were up before morning light.

Lea had taken watch with Tocsen through the night, and he stretched now, working the stiffness out of his muscles by the morning fire. He tilted the big camp pot, pouring himself another cup of coffee.

The Baron was up on time, as usual. Give the squarehead that; you didn't have to pry him out of the soogins every morning. Now, by firelight, he was doing exercises. Lea supposed he had learned to do that kind of thing at officer's school or whatever. Up, down, up, down. Turn this way, turn that way. Up, down, up, down. Now it was time for him to start touching his toes. This was the part that Tocsen liked. Lea watched, smiling, as the old Shoshone, hunkered down by the fire, stared at the big German, watching fascinated while he puffed and grunted, his hind end in the air, trying to touch his toes. It was probably the best part of Tocsen's day.

The Baron, sweating a little in his double-breasted wool outfit, stood tall, stretched out his arms, and took a deep breath. He always ended his exercises the same way. Now, Lea knew, he would have one cup of coffee, black, a half loaf of sourdough bread, and three fried eggs for breakfast. Then he would march out to the latrine ditch, do his duty, and march back. Then he would say *guten morgen,* check his rifle—the Martini-Henry today—get on his stallion, and sit, stiff-backed as a Cheyenne war chief, waiting for Lea to lead off. The Baron was a man of habit.

When Lea led out of camp, the rim of mountains to the east were just touched with red and gold along their peaks. The camp lay still in darkness.

By full dawn, they were high on the plateau, riding up through deep stands of lodgepole pine, the rising sun gleaming gold through their lofty needled tops. The day was cool and still, the wide pale sky arching high from mountain range to mountain range.

They saw mule deer below them, on a dwarf-pine swale along a ridge. A lead buck, then five, maybe six, does.

Lea looked back, and saw the Baron turned in his saddle, watching the deer below. Behind him, the pack horses climbed steadily along, loads swaying a little, heads nodding with the pace.

The Baron looked up and saw Lea watching. He gestured down at the deer, and looked a question at Lea.

Lea shook his head, and the Baron grimaced and nodded as if his suspicions had been confirmed. The German was no fool: he'd noticed the watch the night before, and he'd noticed the tension in Lea as they traveled. And now, no hunting—no rifle shots.

Lea still expected trouble from the drifters, if not by

chase then by ambush.

Lea didn't need to read the squarehead's mind to know what he was thinking. He was thinking that Lea had been a soft-headed fool after all, for not shooting the drifters down as they rode away.

Lea had *known*, as the Baron and old Tocsen must have known, that the drifters were too desperate for mounts *not* to try for the string. There'd been no doubt about it—and no doubt about the kind of men they were, either.

Lea had backed away from doing what had to be done. That dodge might very well cost them when they left High Pass.

He was afraid, and not of the three drifters. He was afraid of a name, and the reputation that went with it. *The West's Premier Gun-man.* That was what that fool Ned Buntline had written. And it might have even been true—once. He had lost too much because of that name, that gun-killer reputation. The man who'd shot down those three drifters in cold blood would have been a marked man, a man to inquire after, to question.

Lea's hands were clenched on his saddle bow; then he jerked roughly at the reins, spurred the startled sidle out of the big dun, and rode up the ridge at a run, waving reassurance to the pack train behind him as he went. He needed time to think.

He rode to the top of the ridge; from there, looking down, he could see the stands of gold-leaved frost-touched aspen. Then, at an angle by timbers fallen from an old lightning fire, he saw the crawling dots of the pack-train coming up. Four small dots in a landscape.

He swung off the dun, looped the reins around the bushy tip of a dwarf pine, and went over to a bed of

27

pine needles lying rich and light brown in the morning sunlight. He took off his hat, lay down, and tucked the high-crowned gray Stetson under his head for a pillow.

He didn't have any more thinking to do; he realized that even as he stretched out, easing his muscles in the soft, aromatic warmth of the pine bed. It was all decided already, had been while he was riding up.

He'd hired on to guide. He'd taken the job, and that was that. The squarehead Baron was his responsibility —the same as if it was Lily Langtry herself he'd taken hunting from Gunstock. He'd signed on with old Abe Bridge to take care of Bridge's people on the hunts. And that was what he would do.

If the drifters made their try—it would be near sunset before the pack-string could make it through the pass— then so much the worse for them. And if a certain secret, a personal thing, got known because of that, then it would be known. He'd run before. He could run again.

Lea lay resting for a while, watching high, white mare's tails sailing over the Bitteroot peaks, clouding in from the west. Storm—but not tonight. Tomorrow, maybe. *By this time tomorrow,* he thought, *we'll be high on the hog up at Gunstock,* or we'll be dead.

Soon after, he heard the click and clack of the horses' hooves. The string had caught up to him.

He got up, walked over to the dun and swung aboard, turned the horse's head, and trotted to meet the string.

"We'll pull up and rest the horses at the base of the next ridge," Lea said to the Shoshone. "Cold coffee and cold elk meat, Baron; I want us up into that pass before sunset." The Baron tilted his head up to look. So did

Lea. Another ridge, laced with zig-zags of lodgepole pine, rose above them. Beyond that rose another ridge, granite, with ice and snow streaking its sheer faces. Its towering slabs shone and flashed as the morning sunlight struck the ice. Behind, and higher yet, was Collier's Hill.

It was one of the highest mountains in the range, snowcapped at all seasons, with storms of sleet in midsummer, arctic blizzards in all other seasons. Since Gunstock opened, seven dudes had tried to Swiss-climb their way to the summit. Three of them were still up there.

High Pass cut just below the shoulder of the mountain, below the worst of the storms, Lea hoped. And if it was a dangerous traverse, it was also a short one. An hour should see them over the crest of the mountain's saddle, down into the valley, and Gunstock beyond.

It was never smart to hurry in the mountains. But this time, at least so far, the mountains had let them get away with it.

They'd rested the horses at the base of Cook Stove ridge. Lea and the Baron had drunk cold coffee, and eaten cold elk and sourdough sandwiches. Then they'd gotten back on the trail. Cook Stove went pretty easily. A pack pulled loose going down the other side, and it took some hard work to recover what they could and lash it up again, but no one was hurt, and nothing lost that they couldn't spare.

The worst trouble came in the afternoon, in a field of scree midway up the long slope of Big Bump. It was higher than the first ridge had been, and rougher, a rubble of granite and ice.

The Baron's bay stallion, a shifty heller named Blixen, pulled the kind of trick Lea had been expecting since he'd seen the horse prancing around the stable yards at Gunstock. They had just entered the field of scree, picking their way slowly through the jumble of fallen ice and boulders, when suddenly, right under the hooves of the Baron's stallion, a chickeree, one of the small brown mountain squirrels, came flashing out, chattering and mad as hell. The little animal must have had some nest or burrow there.

Instantly, all hell broke loose.

The bay stallion reared in panic, misstepped, and fell over, rolling. Lea, seeing it happen from a few yards ahead, spun the dun and spurred back, ready to shoot the stallion fast if the Baron were stirrup-caught.

The Baron had been damn lucky. The stallion had hit hard on its shoulder, kicked and rolled. The Baron had been thrown almost twenty feet from the fall, in a deep bank of reddish, mineral-stained snow. The snow was a leftover drift from last year's late winter fall. It was rotten and mushy stuff, hard on the Baron's fancy blue wool suit, but pretty easy on the Baron. Nothing, bar a few scratches and bumps, hurt, but his pride. And that had been marred plenty already.

The big man had heaved himself out of the snowdrift cursing a blue streak in what sounded like very vulgar German. He'd charged up to the bay stallion, which was standing trembling from the fall, and kicked the nervous horse hard in the ass. It had taken some high kicking, but the Baron had got it done. Lea had never liked the German better.

With grim determination, the Baron remounted the

bay, said something in German to him, and moved out across the scree as if nothing had happened. The kick seemed to have done the big bay some good, because the stallion moved off as steady as a railroad train, and gave the Baron no more trouble at all.

They reached High Pass well before dark. At least before the rest of the mountains were dark. High Pass was as black as a closed woodshed, and freezing cold.

They had just cleared the last field of stones, high above Big Bump, when they saw the pass. The huge, towering gateway of black basalt loomed a thousand feet above them, and the trail up to that monstrous split in the mountain chain was wide as a fine Chicago avenue, but broken, heaped and piled by landslides and avalanches until it seemed like a road into hell.

Lea didn't stop to rest men or horses. He rode back to the string, picked a coil of long lead line off a horse pack, and spurred back to the Baron.

"Fasten this lead to Ranger's bridle, Baron," he said, "and lead him out. Tocsen'll follow up the rear and push 'em along."

For a moment, Lea thought the big German was going to argue with him. Then the Baron nodded with a grunt and took the lead rope.

When the pack string was roped up, the Baron riding lead, old Tocsen riding pusher, Lea waved them on, turned the dun's head to the pass, and trotted forward, picking a track. The closer he rode up that slanting causeway of rubble, the harder the wind blew—howling down from the massive peak above. Halfway up, it was black as night, and icy wind and sleet lashed Lea and the staggering dun. The big horse kept trying to turn back, to put his tail to the blizzard wind, but Lea

31

held him in hard, and spurred him on, scrambling over the sharp-edged scree.

Holding his hat brim down in the gusting wind, Lea turned in the saddle, straining for a look at the pack string. Nothing. Nothing but the murderous cold and white sleet on black wind. High above, he heard the mountain's distant grumble, the dangerous talking of tons of rock, weighted and rotten with snow. He turned forward again, bent his head into the gale, and spurred the big dun on. Once, a few yards farther on, he felt the horse's hooves strike a sheet of ground ice— felt the slip and slide as the dun flailed for footing, missed it—and then took hold and strove back up to solid rock.

The wind from the peak began to buffet back and forth, shifting, changing directions. Far ahead, Lea began to see a faint gray glow, a lighter shade of darkness.

Falling stones, knocked loose from the wall of rock above hissed down nearby, cracking and exploding yards away as they struck the granite shelf. Lea saw daylight, just a shimmer, a touch of blue. The wind thundered past him. The icy darkness began to fade. And the dun, picking up its head, champed the bit and sidled, then bucked and broke into a run, down the dim last yards of the pass, and out into the sunlight.

Gunstock valley lay beyond, dark green with dense pine. It stretched below for a dozen miles to the distant foothills that the huge hotel loomed over. It was sunset; the shadows streamed long across the valley floor. They would be home by moonrise. Unless pigtail knew these mountains.

* * *

Lea sat the tired dun just below the pass, waiting for the others to follow him out. Knowing that if they didn't, he'd be riding back in to find them.

He waited for eleven minutes, by the big old silver-backed hunter he tugged from his vest pocket.

Then Baron the Graf Rudiger von Ulm und Felsbach came riding down out of the pass.

He was leading the pack string behind him, and both the Baron and his bay stallion looked a little the worse for wear. As Lea watched, the last of the pack horses—the slab-sided Candy Cane—came skittering down the pass. Then old Tocsen showed, drumming his fat pony's sides with his moccasins, his toothless mouth wide open in some Shoshone song or other.

Lea waved his hat, not wanting to yell. They saw him and slowly worked their way down to the edge of the lumber-slash where he waited. The hotel was of native stone, but many of Gunstock's out-buildings had been cut from this timber. The slash was nearly a quarter-mile wide, littered with fallen timber and clumps of pine too small to have been worth the trouble of cutting.

Lea gave them a short rest there, giving the horses a breather. The Baron didn't have anything to say about High Pass, but he looked a little pale. That ruddy color had faded out a bit. Lea gave them an extra couple of minutes, then he swung up onto the dun.

"Get your weapons out," he said. "We'll be snaking through this fallen timber fast. I'm taking us around the south edge there. If those three made it here before us —and they could have—they'll be waiting for us along the track. Cutting over south might fox 'em."

When Lea finished, the Baron muttered something in

German, and reached down to haul the long Martini out of his saddleboot. Tocsen yawned, and reached behind him for the double-barrel Greener. He'd tied it with cord under the cantle of his saddle.

"You set?" Lea said.

The Baron grunted. The old Shoshone just looked away over the timbered slash, and yawned again.

"Then we *go!*" Lea yelled. And he spurred the dun hard, lining out through the cut timber at a wild gallop, jumping fallen logs, running full out through the scrub pine.

The Baron, the pack-train, and Tocsen came thundering after him.

He was halfway through the slash already, the dun running handy through the broken wood. Lea used his fronted Sharps to ward off branches whipping at him as he went. He wished for a Henry, or some other carbine for this work; it wasn't going to be range shooting if it came to shooting, not in this scrub. And the Sharps was a distance piece.

Lea glanced back. The Baron was coming fast, riding hard in his tall, stiff-backed fashion, and behind him, the pack string and old Tocsen churned along.

Pig tail hadn't known these mountains, after all.

Just as Lea thought it, and started to rein the dun down into the dusk-shade of the uncut pines, a shot rang through the timber. The Baron swayed in his saddle and pitched out headlong into the brush.

CHAPTER FOUR

Lea saw him fall, spun the foaming dun, and spurred him out into the timber slash again. He felt a quick rush of air past his face as he rode. The rifle's crack sounded to the left.

Lea kept the dun lined out for the patch of pine scrub where the Baron had gone down. He drove the laboring dun into the scrub, lifted his foot out of the stirrup, swung his leg over, and lit running, the pine branches whipping at him, the big Sharps balanced in his hands. A third rifle slug snapped through the scrub.

Lea tripped in the tangle and went down hard. He rolled, and was up on his feet again, running. He saw the flash of dark blue in the green of pine. The Baron. He was alive.

The big man was sitting up, his broad, meaty face dead white, the left side and sleeve of his fancy wool suit soaked black with blood. The Martini-Henry was lying across his lap.

He looked up and said something to Lea in German. Lea didn't have time for it. He'd heard a branch breaking from the left, way out. The shooter was coming in.

Lea jumped up a short staircase of splintered logs. The setting sun flashed bright gold into his eyes. In the dazzle, two hundred yards away, he saw a silhouette come leaping. It was pigtail.

Lea got ready to kill him, as he'd done many times before. He raised the Sharps slowly, letting the long heavy muzzle drift, swing, and find its way to pigtail as he came running out of the golden sunlight.

Pigtail was up on the tilted end of a big pine log, still almost two hundred yards out. Standing there, drawing a bead with some kind of lever action. A perfect target. And perfectly safe.

Lea had jammed the muzzle of the Sharps with dirt when he'd fallen. He dropped the big rifle—he'd always hated gunfighting with rifles, the God-damned things. He drew the Colt, steadied it with both hands, and tried a shot. Miss. Just too far.

Pigtail's silhouette shifted, and he fired. He was a good shot. The round smacked into the log beside Lea's hand—a spray of splinters stung his cheek.

Lea turned to try for the Baron's Martini-Henry, and saw the Baron standing tall on a rough pine stump just behind him, the Martini to his shoulder, his bloody left hand gripping the long fore-stock.

"Get down, you damn fool!"

Too late. The Baron, blood dripping from his sleeve, swayed on that uncertain footing, steadied himself, drew his bead, and fired.

The round boomed past Lea's head. He turned just in time to see pigtail—a black stick figure against the flaming setting sun—spin like a dancer and go down,

36

pitching off the end of the log into the brush below.

"Todt!" said the Baron with great satisfaction, and he sagged, swayed, and fell forward full length on his face.

Lea holstered the colt and jumped down to help him. Then, a pleasant high-pitched boy's voice stopped him cold.

"Good shootin, for a dude."

The kid.

Lea turned slowly, and saw the boy standing near a heap of discarded pine slab, maybe twenty, twenty-five feet away.

The boy carried a Spencer carbine balanced in his right hand down by his side. His big Smith & Wesson .44 was still holstered. He hadn't even bothered to cover Lea when he came in. Very fast. Or very stupid.

He didn't look like a stupid boy.

"Looks like he's out," the boy said, glancing down at the Baron. "Out, or dyin'." He looked up at Lea with a smile. "But he sure stopped old Bobby's clock."

So the pigtail's name had been Bobby.

"Just like I'm goin' to stop yours, Dad," the boy said, still smiling.

The Spencer didn't even move. Lea saw that the boy was pistol proud, intended to kill him with the Smith & Wesson.

"Listen to me, son," Lea said. "Just turn around and walk away. And call that other friend of yours, and tell him the same."

The boy's smile widened.

"Listen to me, now, damn it! I'm trying to give you a break!"

The boy laughed aloud. "Goodbye, old man," he said.

Just then—only a stone's throw away to the right—the swift blast and boom of a pistol and shotgun fire mingled.

Tocsen. And the third man.

The boy didn't let it shake him. He was a very cool hand, for so young.

He went for his gun, still laughing a little.

His left hand snapped around to the butt of the .44 like a stockwhip's lash—straight across his narrow belly in a classic cross draw.

It was one of the best that Lea had ever seen. The boy was a natural gun, no doubt about it. And if he'd known to put a little curve into his reach, he might have been even as fast as John Ringo had been. The .44 was coming out in a flash of blued steel.

Lea drew and shot the boy square in the stomach.

The impact knocked him staggering back. He squeezed off a wild shot and the round went smacking into the ground past Lea's right foot. The boy tried to steady himself, to plant his feet, but they wouldn't work for him; the bullet had drilled straight through his lean belly and hit his spine and broken his back. He collapsed against a pine stump, folding up like a carpenter's rule, throwing a long angular shadow across the timber litter beside him.

He sat there, half on his side, and still he tried to bring the Smith & Wesson to bear. A game boy.

Lea shot him in the chest, going for the heart. But the boy slid sideways as he fired, and the slug slammed into the boy's chest.

The boy screamed then, like a hurt child, and the .44 flew out of his hand, forgotten. He thrashed down onto his side, turning, convulsing, trying to crawl away from the agony.

The boy screamed again, trembling in spasms of agony, his face contorted, red as a wailing baby's.

Lea bent over to him and put the muzzle of the Colt behind the boy's jerking head.

Suddenly, vomit came up into Lea's mouth with a rush. It filled his mouth, bitter as gall, and spewed out. He turned aside for a moment, retching.

The air was split by the ringing blast of a shotgun. The boy's head dissolved into rags. A spray of clay-colored brains struck the pine stump with a sudden spatter. Silence. No screams. Lea vomited hard, leaning out to keep it from his trousers and boots.

Tocsen stood watching him, expressionless. Then, he reached down to his shell belt, pulled two buckshots out, and glanced down to reload the Greener.

Lea retched empty, gasped for breath, and slowly straightened up, the Colt still clutched in his hand.

"Other one," Tocsen said. "He I shoot in leg. He goes still back to get a horse from us."

Lea cleared his throat and spit. "You're doing so damn good today," he said to the old man. "Why didn't you go after him and finish him off, too."

The old man shook his head. "He too good shot with pistol. I don't follow him more. You want; you follow."

The old man looked down at the headless boy, and then at the Baron, lying flat out on his face. Lea thought the Baron was still breathing.

He knelt down beside the Baron, and gently turned the big man over. The big German was unconscious, bloody, pale as snow—and alive.

"Get that damned suit off him, and bind that

39

wound!''

The old Shoshone nodded.

"I'm going after the other one."

Lea left the old man working over the Baron's still figure. Reloading the Colt as he went, he trotted off to the right, back toward the line of untimbered trees. It would be where the horses, scared and turned loose, would gather. Where a wounded man would work his way to get them. Damn old Tocsen for not finishing him. The smiling man must have come real close with that one shot, to have made the old Shoshone get so sensible. He wasn't interested in white-man's trouble.

The Baron. The big man could die yet. He was bleeding hard. Damn those three—that boy.

Lea was trying to find the spot he'd heard that shooting from. The old Shoshone didn't lie: If he'd said he'd hit that pilgrim, then he'd hit him.

After he'd cast around in the soft dusk light for a few minutes, quartering the ground, Lea found it. A spray of darkening blood across a patch of brown pine needles. The smiling man was in trouble.

Lea moved out through the fallen timbers, moving fast past the tangles, scrap slides, and deadfalls. He had perhaps half an hour before dark to find the man. Find him, and take or kill him, and then get the Baron to Gunstock before he bled to death.

The long shadows were already fading through the timber, sinking into the soft gray before darkness fell. If the smiling man weren't where Lea thought, if he hadn't tried for a fresh horse, then Lea had lost him, and the man could wait until they tried to move the Baron out, then take his shots from hiding. Lea had to find him, and find him fast.

The blood disappeared. The man had used his bandanna, perhaps torn his shirt for a hasty bandage, anything to stop the telltale bleeding from that wounded leg. Buckshot. It must be hurting like hell.

A horse whinnied. Well ahead, a good hundred yards off at the edge of the pine woods. The smiling man was trying for a horse.

Lea began to run, angling through the tangle, headed for the horse, bulling through the scrub where he could, jumping it, skirting around it where he had to. He didn't try to be quiet about it. The time for that was past.

He pulled up short, still a stone's throw from the forest line, and stood, controlling his breathing, listening hard.

Lea put his fingers to his lips and whistled, loud and long. Instantly, he heard the shuffle and stomp as the big dun, yards away, tried to move toward him.

Lea moved that way, his Colt still in his holster. He'd never had to draw it before trouble faced him, and rarely before trouble had already started. The only damned blessing of a fast draw.

"Hey!" The voice rang through the darkening woods. "Hey, you people! Let's talk about it!"

The smiler knew his people were gone. He must have seen pigtail go down. Maybe heard the boy screaming. Now, he thought three men were coming for him.

"Hey now!"

Lea didn't answer him. Just keep moving in, carefully. It was getting darker. He circled a little to the left, watching where he put his feet on the rough, scrap covered ground. The smiling man had nothing more to say.

41

At first, seeing just the south edge, Lea thought the little clearing ahead was empty, the horses and drifter farther into the pines.

Then he saw the Baron's stallion. The big bay shifted restlessly, tied to a bent pine branch. Past him, Lea saw the dun's big sand-colored rump, dull in the fading light. The pack horses were hobbled in a bunch, just beyond. The smiling man lay behind a stump a little in front of them. The drifter was stretched along the ground, his right knee bent to ease his wounded leg.

Tocsen and the Greener had done a rare job on that leg. The drifter looked to have tried to bind it with the sleeves torn from his shirt. But it was very bad; the bone had been smashed. There was a small puddle of dark blood under the man's lower leg. A gleam of white bone between the bandages.

The smiling man wasn't smiling now. He was lying still, his face as white as milk, a long-barreled Peacemaker gripped in both hands. He was aiming in the direction Lea had been when he'd whistled.

Lea stepped out into the clearing as quietly as he could. There was a chance—just a chance—to take the man alive.

"Now, put that revolver down right there," he said quietly.

The drifter froze, his face twisted with fear.

"Just put that piece down, and you'll live," Lea said to him. The man had no choice, lying back to him, less than twenty feet away. Meat on the table.

The smiling man had guts. He dropped the Peacemaker, and then, grunting hard at the pain, he slowly struggled until he was standing awkwardly, balanced on his good leg; the other, bleeding, he held just off the ground. He reached out to hold onto a bent pine branch, then looked Lea in the eye. He managed to force a smile.

"The best laid plans of mice and men . . ." he said. "Damn if I thought anybody around these days could kill that kid."

"I'll take you in," Lea said. "A doc'll look after that leg."

"Much obliged," the smiling man said. He gave Lea an odd look, staring at him hard through the gathering darkness. "I . . . " He stared harder, his eyes widening. "Oh, my God!" he said. "Great God almighty, you're *Buckskin* Frank Leslie!"

"I'm sorry, pilgrim," Lea said. "I'm sorry."

And he shot the smiling man through the heart.

CHAPTER FIVE

Sarah heard the orchestra playing the *gallop*, "Garryowen", as she came down the grand staircase. At Gunstock, the balls lasted till one. The *gallop* was always played at midnight. Herr Speyer was in good form tonight, the orchestra sounded wonderful.

Sarah had just spent a very trying half hour in the Blue Suite, trying to comfort an unhappy young Baroness who'd been soundly snubbed by Harry Van Dettler just an hour ago during supper. Harry's father owned half of upstate New York, and Harry, golden blond and six-foot-three, was a great deal too handsome for his own good—or for the good of little Swedish Baronesses.

"Ah, it is indeed my lovely hostess, Miss Sarah Bridge!" Sarah, almost at the bottom of the staircase, glanced down. Count Yuri Orloff, at the foot of the stairs, stook looking up at her. The Count was a small, neat young man, with smooth, pitch-black hair, and a rakish cavalry mustache. His almond eyes were black as well, and seemed to glitter in the bright haze of candlelight.

Count Orloff, as old Abe had put it to his daughter, had the worst damn reputation in Czar Nicholas's court. And that, he added, was saying a "by-God-damn big say!" When the Count's carriage—shipped ahead of him a month in advance to Truckee, thirty miles down the mountains—when that blazoned carriage, shining with trappings of silver and gold, had thundered up the long drive to Gunstock, escorted by half a dozen bearded Cossack savages who rode their black horses like Cheyenne, Sarah, waiting on the wide granite staircase to welcome their guest, had felt an odd chill that had nothing to do with the fresh bite of the mountain wind.

To be sure, the handsome young Count had been nothing but courtesy itself. Always polite, always attentive, as if, for him, there could be no one so fascinating as a tall, slightly awkward girl, the daughter of a rough old prospector who'd struck it rich and opened a luxury hotel.

The Count paid her a great deal of attention, and he smiled. But Sarah had seen him once, from her bedroom window, when one of his horses had bucked and kicked out at him as he prepared to mount it in the stableyard below.

The Count had stepped back from the animal, smiling, and had made a little sign with his hand to the two Cossacks who stood by him. One of them, a black-bearded giant named Grigori, had walked to the horse, uncoiling from his shoulder the long-lashed braided whip the Cossacks all carried, and as Sarah watched from above, flinching, her hand over her mouth, and whipped the screaming horse until it bled

45

in streams onto the stable stones.

The news of that had gone around the great hotel in a flash, and Sarah had begged old Abe to throw the Count out of Gunstock, Cossacks, carriage, whips and all! But Abe had just shaken his head. They'd had cads and bounders and roughs at Gunstock before. And he knew —and Sarah should know—that the swells were, if anything, a wilder trade than a riverside inn's. The Count was richer than a dozen robber barons—except for Tom Larreby, maybe—and if he chose to mistreat a horse, well, it was his damn horse.

Sarah couldn't bring herself to tell her father that she was afraid of the man. Old Abe would have been amazed, and embarrassed, to think that anything or anybody could frighten a daughter of his. And Count Orloff had never done anything, never said anything to her that wasn't the pleasantest compliment.

It was what was unsaid, what was in his eyes, that frightened her.

"May I say, Miss Sarah," the Count said, "that that blue gown is a perfect compliment to your eyes."

"Thank you, Count," Sarah said, "You're most flattering." And she stepped to the bottom of the staircase and tried to go past him.

"But Miss Sarah," he said, and his slender white hand reached out to gently grip her arm. "Will you not honor me with a waltz? Just one?"

Sarah tried to pull away, but the white hand closed on her arm with a slow and dreadful power. She felt her arm numb to the wrist from that viselike grip. The Count seemed to have the strength of a man twice his size.

"My waltz?" he said.

Sarah turned to face him, her eyes blazing.

"Let go of my arm, damn you, or I'll hit you in the face!"

The Count's bright black eyes widened, and he grinned.

"You do not disappoint me, my dear savage," he said. And he let her go. "Another time, perhaps." He bowed. "When you know what it is that you *really* want."

Sarah turned her back and walked away across the great two-storied hall, feeling her heart pounding as she went. At the wide double doors to the ballroom, she paused to compose herself.

I won't tell father . . . I won't! That smiling bully! To put his hand on me that way! She took a deep breath, and stepped forward into the ballroom.

It was a sea of gold and crimson. More than a thousand candles—Sarah knew their cost to the penny —blazed along the walls. And the walls, covered in rich crimson velvet, seemed on fire in the light. Three-hundred couples, the men in fine black broadcloth and snowy linen, or in the uniforms of a dozen armies: all blue, or red, or white and gold. The women were moving fairylands of velvets, silks, and lace. Diamonds, rubies, and sapphires sparkled at their breasts, and ropes of pearls gleamed on white throats and shoulders as they swayed and swung around and around in the dance.

Ball night at Gunstock. Leo Drexel's pride and joy. Leo Drexel had been a scion of Philadelphia society, until some old scandal involving a handsome young groom had necessitated his removal to, as he put it, "more rustic purlieus." Whatever his oddities, Drexel had been a godsend to old Abe Bridge. It was Leo Drexel who had instructed the tough old prospector exactly how to attract, entertain, and generally cater to what he called "The Great World," by which, Leo meant the rich—titled if possible, but always rich.

"A Palace in the Wilderness," he'd said to old Abe. "That's what you want to create. A palace, a resort, a spa, a gambling den"—old Abe had pricked up his ears at that—"a place to see, and to be seen. A place, above all, that's *expensive!*" Leo Drexel of Philadelphia, and Abe Bridge of Silver City and points west, had understood each other very well.

Now, Leo had his suite in the south wing, a very handsome, if somewhat sullen young Peigan Indian as "body servant," and an occupation that consisted almost entirely of giving parties—the more splendid the better—for the guests of Gunstock.

And if many of the parties ended in the small hours at the tables of the ornate little Gunstock casino overlooking the wide back terrace, and a hundred miles of moonlit mountains, so much the better.

Sarah was well aware, since she acted as her father's accountant, as well as hostess and housekeeper-in-chief, that without the casino, Gunstock would soon be bankrupt. And even the casino didn't bring in the money that it might have, thanks to old Abe's habit of giving in to the pleas of some of the casino's losers—young adventuresses, and desperate young men with grim fathers in businesses in Boston, London, and New York. Faced with these white young faces, tearful and strained, old Abe would all too often heave himself up out of his fine leather wing chair, stump across his study—decorated for him in books and animal hides by Leo Drexel—open the safe, take out the young unfortunate's losings, and return them with a pained roar. "Hear, damn it! Take the damn stuff back!"

48

This earned the old man a great deal of gratitude. But it cost Gunstock a pretty penny from time to time. A penny that huge resort could ill afford to lose.

A young man named Easterby, a second son of the Earl of March, came up to Sarah, smiling. Toby Easterby was out in the American west on his father's business—the Earl had considerable holdings in Wyoming and Idaho—and for his own pleasure. He was a short square-built young man with reddish hair. A nice young man.

"Hullo, Sarah. Good god, what a crush you have here! I've been going mad waiting for you to introduce me to that Austrian creature!"

The 'Austrian creature' was a handsome blonde woman, several years older than Toby Easterby, known as Giesela von Rhune. Sarah suspected the lady changed her name and her title whenever it suited her. Her taste in men appeared to run to older, very substantial types, all very rich, none of them second sons.

"Isn't she a little . . . well . . . a little . . ."

"Old for me?" said Toby, who regarded Sarah as more of a sister than another young lady. "Not a bit. She's just my style, Sarah." He flushed a little. "But you wouldn't understand."

The notion that, having practically run a great resort hotel and casino, catering to the fastest sets in Europe and the East, she should not understand, struck Sarah as funny.

"No, I don't suppose I do," she laughed; and took Toby Easterby in tow, threaded around the circling dancers with him, and finally located the very handsome von Rhune in animated conversation with a sixty-year-old banker—a recent widower—from Baltimore.

49

The lady was not greatly pleased to be introduced at just that moment to young Toby Easterby. She knew— as she knew about every eligible man in the room— exactly what young Easterby's prospects were, and she found the elderly, and very rich, Mr. Blalock far more attractive.

She gave Sarah a quick, cold look, smiled brilliantly upon Toby, and sent him off, happy as a clam, to get lemonade for her. Lemonade, this evening. Mr. Blalock was a teetotaler.

Sarah had just turned back to cross the wide room to the band—when Leo Drexel came up to her, tall, thin, elegant, and annoyed.

"Well, there you are!" he said. "I've been scouring this barn trying to track you down. Your impossible father is tangled in a billiards game and won't listen to a word I say! Some creature from the stables has been lurking at the back entrance whining for Abe to come and see. To come and see *what,* the creature wouldn't tell me!"

"I'll go," Sarah said.

"And what, in heaven's name, is old Speyer doing to that Meyerbeer? He's been asked to play Strauss twice, and by people who could buy and sell this place!"

Sarah left the ballroom, turned down the broad hallway, and walked toward the maze of back passageways commencing under the massive main staircase.

She went to a narrow door deep in the shadows at the end of the hall, opened it, stepped down a flight of stairs to a short hallway, and walked out into Gunstock's servants' dining room. There was no one there except one of the upstairs maids, a short, pretty little

50

turkey from the remains of supper upstairs.

The girl got to her feet when she saw Sarah, and bobbed her a curtsy.

"Can I help you, Miss Bridge?"

"No, no, Edna, go on with your supper."

Sarah went to the big closet by the door, opened it, and searched through the hanging waiters' jackets, maids' uniforms, and cooks' smocks for something to use as a wrap. Finally, she found one of Mrs. Parker's old shawls, wrapped it around her shoulders, and started out of the dining room.

"Edna, if anyone needs me, I've gone out to the stables."

"I'll tell 'em, Ma'am," the girl said, and stood waiting until Sarah had left the room to sit down again to her supper.

Sarah walked through the noise and steam and bustle of the huge kitchen, nodding and smiling to an incomprehensible remark shouted across the tumult by the immensely fat Monsieur de la Maine, head chef of Gunstock, and a testy, very talented tyrant. No guest who came to Gunstock ever left complaining of the food. She pushed open the heavy kitchen back door.

The mountain night was as cold as spring water, and pitch dark. The moon was just visible through the thick branches of the tall ponderosas that rose from the border slopes of the back lawns. Its soft silver light barely filtered through their dense, dark foliage.

Sarah had just started down the flagstone path beside the terrace wall, when a hulking figure stepped out of the dark into her path to block her way.

She drew back, clutching the shawl to her throat.

"Who are you? What do you want?"

"Miss Bridge, ma'am?"

Sarah relaxed, feeling her heart still thumping. It was

51

only Tiny Morgan, Frank Budreau's stable hand—a huge, gentle half-wit, and the butt of Budreau's occasional, cruel practical jokes.

"Yes, Tiny? What is it?"

She saw the gigantic figure, in dark silhouette against the deeper darkness of the night, respectfully remove its hat and shuffle awkwardly at addressing the boss's daughter.

"Well, ma'am, Frank . . . he sent me to tell the boss. Tell him there's trouble, Frank said. Right down in the stables."

"What kind of trouble, Tiny?"

"Oh . . . bad!" the huge shadow said. "Shootin' trouble!"

Sarah began to be sorry that she hadn't gotten her father out of his billiards game after all. Abe had a short way with any gun play or troublemaking. She thought of going back inside to get him. But, no! She'd run enough this evening. That nasty Russian had sent her scurrying into the ballroom like a cottontail, and she was damned if she'd make a habit of scooting.

"Well, Tiny. . . what are you waiting for? Let's go see that trouble!"

She followed the stablehand's dark bulk along the great length of the terrace wall. Above them, through the closed French doors, she heard the rythmic sounds of the orchestra.

Tiny led her to the end of the terrace wall, then turned off down the path to the stables. The path led down through the gardens, and Sarah looked across the moon-bleached flowerbeds to the small fountain splashing bravely away against the looming backdrop of the Bitteroots, their snow-streaked peaks gleaming in soft starlight.

Tiny walked before her out onto the scrubbed

cobbles of the stableyard. Most of the rough cedar buildings were dark, but a single bright beam of lantern-light shone out across the stones from a half-open door in the carriage house.

Sarah brushed past the lumbering stablehand, and hurried toward the light. The doctor, she was thinking. If someone is hurt, surely Budreau has had the sense to send for Dr. Edwards. Edwards was a young Yale man. A fine physician, she supposed, though he seemed more interested in hunting and fishing at Gunstock than his doctoring. He had a brusque way with imagined illnesses, but his good looks kept him popular with the older ladies. He was also a *devotée* of the new English sport of *mountaineering,* and had twice tried to climb Collier's Hill.

Sarah pushed the carriage-house door wide open, and stepped into the light, inhaling the close, smoky smell of an overheated stove. Then she stood still, and the stove's heat seemed to vanish into ice.

Doctor Edwards was bending over a man stretched out unconscious on the broken old rawhide couch the coachmen used. The man's clothes were soaked with blood. It was the Baron.

"Oh, my God!"

Edwards looked up, irritated. "Come in or out, Miss Bridge, but shut the door." He bent over the injured man again. Where's your father?"

"What's *happened* here?" Sarah said, going to the couch.

"He's been shot." Edwards said. "That's what's happened."

"My fault, Miss Bridge."

Standing behind the couch, Farris Lea looked at her, his eyes steady. The rage welled up in her.

She stared at him for a moment, wordless, too angry

53

to speak. And he stood staring back—Tall, filthy in his trail clothes, Unshaven—and staring back at her as if . . .

"Oh! You *saddle bum!*" Her face flamed red with anger. "How *could* you have let this happen!"

She knelt beside the broken sofa.

"Doctor Edwards, just how badly is he hurt?"

Edwards muttered, busily bandaging the German's broad, grizzled chest. "Oh, he'll do. He'll do. Lost a lot of blood."

"The way it happened—" Lea began.

"I don't *care* how it happened," Sarah said through clenched teeth. Looking up, she saw the ugly old Indian that followed Lea around on the hunting trips. The old man was squatting in front of the pot-belly stove, staring into the glow of the cherry-red iron.

"I don't *care* what stupidity has caused this! But I can tell you that this may *ruin* us!" She drew a deep breath, her blue eyes sparkling with anger. "And I can tell you and that Indian of yours to get out of Gunstock—get off our land! And if you don't get out, I'll have our hands *whip* you out!"

CHAPTER SIX

Lea woke an hour before dawn, coming awake with a jolt. He'd been dreaming of the smiling man just as he'd shot him through the heart. Murder. Cold murder, and nothing else.

Someone was scratching at the door of the little cabin he lived in at Gunstock. They'd offered him a separate room in the hand's bunkhouse. He'd refused it. Coming from the stillness, the healing quiet of the mountains, the rowdy noise of twenty Gunstock cowhands would have been no pleasure at all.

He wouldn't have to worry about that anymore. He'd been ordered off the place by Abe's daughter, that bony blue-eyed bitch. And it was probably just as well. Better not even to try to explain what had happened. Leave it a hunting accident, and nobody the wiser.

No questions, then. Wasn't likely anyone'd miss those three drifters. Not soon, for sure.

The scratch on the door came again.

Lea stretched, grunting, on the narrow cot, then threw the Hudson blanket back and swung his legs to the rough puncheon floor. He reached under his pillow, snaked out a Root Sidehammer, and with the small revolver in his hand, strode naked the few steps to the door.

He reached out to slide the bar free, and stepped lightly to the side as the heavy plank door swung open. It was an odd hour for visiting, even with the Baron hurt and the whole place in a quiet uproar about it.

As the door opened, a small white hand reached in from the darkness to grip it, to keep it from opening wider. A girl's slender shape slid into the cabin.

"Oh, close the door, Farris. 'Tis cold as blue blazes outside!"

Lea frowned into the darkness, swung the door shut, and barred it.

"Edna."

He'd been screwing the little Irish maid for months—and so, probably, had a large number of the male guests at Gunstock. But he sure as hell wasn't in the mood this morning. Even as the girl leaned against him in the dark, he heard the echo of the smiling man's voice. "The best-laid plans of mice and men . . ."

"Listen, Edna, I'll be leaving pretty soon this morning."

"And don't I know that, my dear," she said, "with the whole grand place in a topsy over it. The missus is that angry about it! That poor old German."

One of her small, cold hands slid down Lea's naked side, stroked, reached to feel his cock, grip it, squeezing.

"I've got to be out of here by first light, Edna," Lea said, pushing her away gently.

"Ah, no . . . ah, no, now." The girl began to move

56

her hand on him. The small fingers, warmer now with the cabin's heat, curling, tugging at him.

Lea felt his cock stiffening, growing slowly fat and hard in her grip.

"There now . . . there now."

"You want it that bad, you little bitch?"

"Ah, yes . . . yes, I do, you dirty man." Her other hand was on him now, tugging, massaging, squeezing. He felt her breath hot on the bare skin of his chest.

He'd first had her behind the stable, the second month he'd been at Gunstock. The small, black-haired Irish girl had been drunk and laughing, full of whiskey from one of the late-night stable dances the Gunstock hands used to run once a month, in rough imitation of the swell's balls up at the hotel.

Edna had staggered up to him, her round, white face flushed, and announced she needed a strong man to take her out behind the stable "for a vomit, dearie."

She'd reminded Lea of the half savage, wild-haired Irish gandy-dancers he'd seen. A fierce, tough, crude little peasant girl, all overlaid—for her employers—with the meek and respectful air they expected in a parlor maid. She was the wildest and most beautiful of the dozens of little Irish girls who dusted, and mopped, cleaned and linened the endless rooms and corridors of the great hotel. Between these girls and the hardcase cowhands old Abe hired to run the Gunstock cattle, after hours tended to become a little lively.

Lea had fended off a dead-drunk cowpoke, taken the small girl by the arm, and steered her out into the winter night. He'd been a little drunk, himself. Too drunk to give a damn about the cold, or anything else. It had been weeks since he'd had a woman.

Edna had shivered in the cold; she was wearing only a shawl and a cheap spotted gingham dress. She'd stumbled over against the stable wall, thrown her shawl back out of the way, bent over, and vomited her guts out into the snow.

Lea was impatient, hot and angry, and in no mood to wait. As the girl was bent over, retching, he'd stepped up behind her, reached down to pull her long skirts up, gathered the flowing material up in one hand, and reached down again to grip the soft, cool rounds of her ass. He'd squeezed her hard, digging his fingers into the hot softness between her cheeks.

Edna had gasped with shock, had tried to straighten up, to pull away from him.

"I'm sick," she said. "I'm sick."

Lea'd paid no attention. He'd probed, shoving his fingers up between her legs, into the fat pout of fur— slid his forefinger up and deeper, until he'd felt the soft line of dampness and then dug his finger into her.

She'd cried out and tried to struggle, but Lea had gripped the back of her neck and held her hard.

He'd gotten his cock out, forced her against the stable wall, and bucked hard against her naked ass, driving his cock into her with one savage thrust. Surrounded by the snow and icy air, he'd felt the sudden wet and heat of her cunt clutch at him as she'd cried and tried to twist away.

He'd held her there, and fucked her hard, winding her long black hair in his fist to keep her still.

She'd yelled, and cursed him.

"There, now . . ."

He was up, fully hard.

"That's what it is I want." She went up on tiptoes in the dark to kiss him, licking at his lips, thrusting her wet little tongue into his mouth.

Both her hands were on him, gripping him hard.

"All right, you little bitch . . ."

Lea reached down, gathered the small girl up in the darkness, and carried her over to the bed. Then he dropped her onto the cot, held her while she squirmed impatiently, and peeled the long dress up and off her. He snapped the lacings of her cheap corset, pulled it away, and swung his leg over to straddle her, gripping her round little breasts hard enough to make her whimper. Then he bent down in the dark to kiss her deeply, getting his tongue into her, drinking from her as if the girl were a cup of sweet water.

Edna groaned, moving under his weight, her small hands rough on the hot skin of his swollen cock. He felt her thumb rubbing at the tip, smearing the heavy shaft with the slippery oil leaking from it.

"Ah, darlin' . . . me darlin' . . . I want ya . . . do me, darlin', before you'll be goin' away."

Lea slid his hands down the silky length of her thighs, soft as down over the neat smooth muscles of years of woman's work. He hooked his thumbs behind the soft bend of her knees, and forced her legs up and out, spreading her. He put his hand down in the darkness, and found her there, hairy, hot, and wet.

He smelled the faint, salty, meaty odor of her. And he pushed a finger into her.

The girl grunted. Lea heard the soft wet sounds as his finger moved in deep. He put a second finger into her and she heaved up against him on the creaking cot.

"You like it, don't you, you little whore?"

59

"Ohhh . . . oh, yes. I do like it, oh, you dirty man."

Lea took his hand away from her and hitched up higher on the cot, crouching over her in the dark. He slid his hand to the back of her neck, gripped it, and pulled her head up. He held his swollen cock with his other hand, and pressed the hot, aching tip of it against her face, rubbing it hard across her lips.

"Mmmm . . ."

He felt her breath against him. Then, the soft, warm, wetness of her tongue. He felt her lapping at the bulging tip, lapping at it like a cat. He heard the quick liquid sounds of it in the dark.

Slowly, Lea forced his cock into the girl's mouth. She tried to resist, to turn her head away, but he wouldn't let her. He shoved the swollen head of it into her mouth. He felt the wetness, the heat, the slight stinging scrape of her teeth as she struggled to take it all.

She wanted it now. She wanted all she could get.

He kept slowly driving the length of it into her, as she licked at it, sucked it like a hungry baby, making desperate, thirsty sounds in the close darkness of the cabin.

He had the head of it in her now, and some of the stiff, veined shaft. He felt her tongue moving frantically against it, the touch of her teeth.

He fed her another inch and felt her gag, her soft throat convulsing around the head of it.

"Swallow it, you little bitch."

The smiling man would get no more of this. No girl would moan, gulping on his prick.

If only he'd had sense enough to keep his mouth shut. Sense enough not to say the name . . .

Couldn't a man run far enough, or fast enough, so as

not to have to kill to be left alone?

The little Irish girl thrashed under him, choking, struggling, trying to breathe.

He put another inch into her. It slid right in, deep into her throat. Her throat closed around it, spasming against the wide shaft. He would kill the bitch if he wasn't careful.

Suddenly, Lea pulled away—pulling the length of cock out of the struggling girl's mouth. It was dripping.

She turned away, heaving, gasping for breath— sobbing with the need for air. With fear. Lea bent down to kiss her.

"I'm sorry, pretty girl. I'm sorry . . ."

"That's okay." He felt her soft lips against his cheek. "I know it's you that's sad, poor darlin'."

He began to stroke her breasts, calming her, soothing her, carressing her round little belly.

When she was calm, moving slightly under his hands, Lea bent over her again, and lightly kissed her nipples, sucking gently at the stiff, swollen little buttons of flesh.

She groaned with pleasure, moving restlessly under him. He smelled the sweat on her, now, felt her skin's heat through his hands.

He reached down, gripped her waist, and turned her over on her belly. She went over easily, softly, a small heap of silken flesh. He bent over to press his face against the cool round cheeks of her ass, breathing in the warm earthy smells. The odors of a healthy, sweaty, young girl—fresh from a bath to hot bed work.

He gripped one of her ass cheeks in each big hand. Squeezed them, gently pulled them apart.

Then, while she lay groaning beneath him, Lea bent

down again, and began to slowly, gently lick her spread crotch, licking deep into the soft, furry heat of her, running his tongue up along the hot moist crack of her ass. Licking at the neat little bud of her asshole, then down and in, to the wet, slippery folds of her cunt.

Edna gasped and pulled herself up to her knees, crouching with her head buried in the sweaty pillow, her slim back arched, her round little buttocks gleaming white in the first faint light of dawn.

He spread her ass cheeks wide, and buried his face in her, as if to eat her alive.

CHAPTER SEVEN

She was crying aloud, shoving her little butt back into his face as he worked on her. It was a pimp's trick—butt-licking. And why not? Lea had spent a lot of good years in the Life—no use letting them go to waste. All those years.

Canary, Big Nose Kate, The Yellow Cow, all those tough sweethearts from the cowtowns, and railroad whorewagons, and mine-town parlors. Ugly as sin, most of them. And damn good sports. And a damn good living, too, while it lasted.

Edna was crying, sobbing with the pleasure he was giving her. She was loving it. Shoving her ass back for more. Lea licked his finger, and slowly, carefully, worked the tip of it into the girl's ass. And then twisted it in deeper.

"Oh, Jesus!" She cried out and tried to move away.

"Shhh." He moved the finger farther into her. Slowly, gently. "I won't hurt you, beautiful."

She groaned and turned her head on the pillow. And she thrust her ass back for more.

Lea hunched up behind her, turning his finger in her tight, clenching asshole. He reached down with his other hand, gripped the taut shaft of his cock, and slowly stroked the swollen tip up against her wetness. He felt the soft, furry dampness against him.

He held it, pushed, working under his other flattened hand, the finger still moving in her ass. He felt the moist grip, the hot oil of her cunt, and drove full into her.

"Ahhhh!" Edna screamed with pleasure as the thick length rode slowly into her—shoving, driving deep into her with a rich, liquid sound, until his belly smacked softly against her soft ass, his imprisoned finger.

Lea reached under her crouching body with his other hand to grip and stroke her plump little breasts, to pull and tug at her nipples—at first gently, then harder and harder, until she moaned and murmured with the sweet pain of it.

Now, he was moving over her, faster and faster, smacking into her, his swollen, wet cock pushing deep into her, pulling out, thrusting in again. Edna buried her face in the pillow, groaning, yelping with pleasure as he fucked her, squealing mindlessly as her ass clenched around the slamming pole of his cock, the tickling, twisting finger moving in her ass.

"Ahhh!"

"You like it, Edna? You like it, little whore?"

"Ahh God . . . ahhh . . . Jesus yes . . . oh, I love it!"

Lea pulled his finger out of her, and she screamed when he did it. Then he reached down with both hands to grip her breasts, squeezing them.

She was writhing, slippery with sweat, smelling of salt and fish. Grunting like an animal as he came at her.

He crushed her breasts in his hands, threw back his head blindly, and he came. It rushed out of him, flowed out of him like a river. It burned and soothed and jerked out of his throbbing cock deep into the hot, wet, moving core of her.

Edna's thin scream echoed his gasps as she thrust her round buttocks higher, her soaked, hairly little cunt gaping wide, then clenching as she came.

He felt the firm grip, the heat and softness and swelling around him. He heard her soft whimpers, and felt the small taut body under his soften and relax. She slowly collapsed beneath him, slumping under him into a warm, slippery cushion of girl, softly murmuring her pleasure.

"Your luck isn't bad luck, Farris. 'Tis good luck that you're havin'."

"That so?"

They were lying tangled together on the narrow cot, drowsy and at ease as the gray dawn light slowly brightened in the little cabin.

Lea would have been glad of some quiet just then. Soon, he'd have to be up and going—packing his warbag and saddlebags—going out to saddle the tired dun for the ride out. He wished he could give the big horse another day's graining and stable rest, but it wasn't in the cards, not the way Abe's daughter had sounded last night.

Best to be up and away by full sunrise. No use giving Budreau a chance to sic the hands on him—to hustle him off the place.

Budreau. A bowlegged bully, and stud duck at Gunstock, at least as far as the ranch work went. And the ranch work was a big part of the Gunstock operation, for cash as well as supplies of beef and garden goods for the hotel kitchens.

Budreau hadn't liked Lea's face from the start—hadn't liked him going off hunting with the swells, for money every bit as good as Budreau got for breaking butt with the hands and the cattle.

Budreau was a stocky, bull-chested foreman, with his long-nosed foxy face, his long black hair greased into girlish waves with Macasser oil.

Lea had never seen him wearing a gun. Only a knife—a big broad-bladed Bowie with a point and edge curved like a reaping hook.

A bad one. Lea could smell them. A bad one, gone straight. At least straight enough to ramrod the Gunstock cows to old Abe's satisfaction.

"Are you asleep now, Farris?"

"No. I'm awake."

Edna turned in his arms to kiss him. "Did you hear me, then? About the hotel and all?"

"What about it?"

"Why, the old man and his daughter are to lose it, sure. And then what's to happen to us who work for them, I'd like to know?"

"Lose Gunstock? What are you talking about, Edna?"

She snuggled into his arms.

"Oh . . . I was folding in the linens on the fourth floor last night, by the green suite, you know, and I could hear 'em plain as day, plottin' and plannin' their schemes in there."

"So?"

"Well, it was that nasty old Mr. Larrabee, and that Rooshin . . . that Count what's-his-name!"

66

Lea yawned, stretched, gently untangled himself from the girl, and sat up on the side of the cot.

"Oh, don't go just yet, will ya?"

"I have to, sweetie." He reachd back to stroke her bare leg. "You're a good girl, Edna . . . a good woman."

"I'm a wicked, sinful girl, that's what I am."

He turned and bent down to kiss her. "Never think that, beautiful." Then he stood up and walked naked to the water basin near the small pot-belly stove. He bent, opened the grate, and slid another stick of hickory onto the coals, then he stood at the basin to splash his chest and face and armpits with cold water. He thought of washing his groin, then didn't. He liked the idea of riding off with the sticky love juices still drying on him. It seemed less lonely, to go off that way.

Edna lay sprawled in the sheets, watching him wash and dress. She loved to watch him naked: the long, lean body, roped with muscle, streaked in a half dozen places with the quick white lines of old scars. Scars from fighting, from knives and bullets. She'd seen scars like that on her own father and brothers.

She'd known Lea for a fighting man—a killing gentleman—the first time she'd seen him. And she'd wanted him then.

"You're well out of it. Old Larrabee and that Rooshin Count are surely goin' to steal old Bridge and his daughter blind!" she continued.

Lea sat on the edge of the cot to pull on his boots. "And how's that, Edna?"

"Why, for the silver, man. The silver!"

Lea laughed. "There's no silver in these mountains, girl. And if there was, old Abe would know it."

"That he would not! That Mr. Larrabee told the

67

Rooshin that his railroad surveyors found a fine vein of it showin' in a landslide by Little River!"

"Well, then, so what?"

"Well, Little River is on the Gunstock land, isn't it?" She sat up, tugging the sheet up to cover her breasts. "And that's why they're goin' to take the whole shebang from old man Bridge."

Lea laughed. "And what does the 'Rooshin' have to do with all this?"

Edna pouted. "You go ahead and laugh, then, you brute." She stretched up to bite his ear. "But I'm for tellin' you you're well out of this, lucky to be gone. Because that Rooshin is to make trouble for Mr. Bridge with those nasty Cossacks of his."

Lea walked over to his warbag and began rolling and stuffing his clothes into it. Woolen workstuff, mostly, and one good blue St. Louis suit which he hadn't worn for two years.

Maybe more than two years.

He was listening to Edna with only half an ear. Servant's gossip was plentiful and cheap at resorts like Gunstock. And the notion of old man Larrabee, who'd been a partner of Commodore Vanderbilt's, making common cause with that coldeyed little Russian count in any kind of business, rough or smooth, seemed mighty unlikely.

"Now, what do you say to that, Smarty?"

Lea buckled the warbag shut, and reached up to lift his saddlebags down from the wall peg where they hung.

"And what's in it all for that Russian?" he said. "I hear the man owns a couple of counties over there—and the serfs to go with 'em."

68

"And so he may," Edna said, and stuck out her tongue at him. "But cash money is what his Nibs *don't* have. And Larrabee said he'd give him a million in gold to do his work!"

She lay back on the pillow, thoughtful. Lea could see one small pink nipple peeping over the edge of the sheet.

"I was thinkin' maybe Mister Larrabee'd be grateful to a girl who knows how to keep her trap shut about somethin'." She glanced up at Lea.

He turned to face her, his eyes suddenly cold, and slate-hard.

"I don't know if there's anything to this bull you've told me," he said to the girl. "But if there is anything to it—if you did hear something like that—you better damn well stay away from Larrabee and the Russian, both! Either one of them would break you like a stick if you crossed them at all. Do you understand me?"

"Oh, all right," Edna said sulkily, "I was just thinkin'."

"Don't think about it—and don't do it."

"I said I wouldn't." She looked up at him through her lashes. "Do you have to be goin' now . . . right this very minute?" The sheet slid down farther from her plump breast.

"Right now," Lea said. "Right this minute."

He slung the warbag over his shoulder, picked up the saddlebags and went over to the cot to kiss her goodbye.

He bent awkwardly with the bags, hugged her warm, naked little body, and kissed her. Her tongue slid into his mouth like a snake. She smelled delicious.

"Goodbye, beautiful."

"Oh, Farris," she said. And her face screwed up like a little child as she began to weep great sentimental Irish tears. "Don't go away from me, darlin'."

But he kissed her again, picked up the big Sharps, and walked out the door.

The only man in the stables was Tiny Morgan. Lea had always gotten on well with the giant half-wit, and Morgan greeted him with a broad smile.

"Good morning, Mr. Lea."

"Good morning, Tiny. How's the dun look?"

The big man shook his head. "Oh, your horse is still a little tired, Mr. Lea. You shouldn't ride him today."

"Got to, though. Lead him out, will you, Tiny."

The big man shook his head sadly, and went to get the horse.

When he brought him out, Lea saw that the dun was fit enough, but damn sure not at his best. The big gelding stood quiet while Lea saddled him and strapped the bags behind the cantle. Lea slid the Sharps into the saddle boot.

"I rode you pretty hard, didn't I, fella?" The dun was getting old for that kind of hard riding. *He isn't the only one getting a little old for hard riding,* Lea thought.

"You'll be easy on him today, won't ya' Mr. Lea?" Tiny Morgan said. The big man loved the Gunstock horses. They never made cruel fun of him the way Budreau and the cowhands did.

"I'll be easy on him, Tiny." Lea led the dun out into the morning light. The sunshine streamed gold across the cobbles. He swung up onto the big gelding. "Bye, Tiny," he said.

"Goodbye, Mr. Lea. Good luck."

70

CHAPTER EIGHT

By noon, he was high in the hills to the west of Gunstock, taking the easy way this time. No ride through High Pass.

He'd seen a big grizzly in the morning, rambling and chewing through a thicket of cloudberries. Lea had automatically marked the big bear, working out its territory, its ways in and out of those steep hill slopes, as if he were still a guide with dudes to bring for the trophy.

You're lucky, bear. I won't be by this way again. He was heading for Oregon, then maybe down to California and Mexico. West. But not to San Francisco. Too many people would remember a sport named Leslie. A sport who sometimes had killed people, just to watch them kick.

Lea pulled the dun up on the steep rise of a rocky knob. The country spread out around him like a patchwork quilt. The autumn colors: browns, dull, glowing reds, bright splashes of yellow, streaks of soft pine greens were as good as a painted picture.

Maybe better.

He swung down off the dun, looped the reins to a gnarled pine stub, and loosened the girth. The dun needed the breather; he'd gone pretty good since sunup, with just a water stop at a mountain branch, and a little cooling time after that.

Lea had drunk deep of the icy water running that little branch, rinsed and filled his canteen at it, and wished he'd taken the time to get some bread and cold meat for the trail.

Lea found a flat sun-warmed seat on one of the clusters of small boulders scattered along the crest of the knob. He dug in the side pocket of his buckskin vest for the stub of a stale cigar. One thing he would miss for sure about Gunstock, besides the French cooking, and sweet Edna O'Malley, was the fancy Havanas old Abe had shipped in for the guests. They beat steamboat stogies hollow.

He could forget that now. All of it. The good hunting . . . the good times. He hoped the Baron pulled out of that bullet wound. He'd looked pretty good, considering. But Lea had seen plenty of men looking pretty good who were dead by morning. The Baron had done all right. He'd gotten a good shot at pigtail—and already hit himself. The Baron had done fine.

The sun was hot, this far up in the hills. Autumn or not, the sun came down hard when you were this high. A hot sun, and a cold wind. Mountain autumn.

Well, Oregon'd be a change. Green and rainy there, most places, he'd heard. And Idaho, and the Bitteroots, just something more to remember.

A girl shot dead in a quarrel. Dead long ago, yet alive in the heart. An old drunk horse doctor had said something like that to Lea in Kansas. The old man had been talking about his wife. "Alive in my heart," the old man had said. "Alive to me . . ."

How she would have laughed to see Frank Leslie herding dudes through the Bitteroots. "Good lord, you're worse than Bill Cody!" Alive in the heart.

There was another girl, another place, to be remembered.

A thin little whore, and a tough little town, an Appaloosa stud, and a ranch. A mountain ranch along Rifle River.

Lea stood up, and as he stood, he saw a distant flicker of motion.

He shaded his eyes and stared hard out to the east— toward Gunstock. A thousand feet down, and maybe two, three miles away, something was moving over the crest of a wooded ridge.

A voice sounded just a few feet behind him.

Lea had turned and drawn before he saw who it was. Tocsen.

The old Shoshone stood slouched beside a wind-stunted pine, looking at Lea without much interest, his heavy-lidded old turtle's eyes still as still water.

The old son-of-a-bitch had followed Lea after all. Lea'd thought that Tocsen would drift off on his own. The old man had never given any sign he liked Lea's company, after all.

"What the hell do you want here, old man?"

The Shoshone didn't answer. He stood looking at Lea for a moment more. Then he grunted and gestured to the east. "There is two riders coming."

"Let 'em come. It's nothing to do with me . . ."

"*Is* to do. They come for you. They follow your

way.''

Tocsen turned and walked off down the slope of the knob, stepping along with his easy bow-legged gait, his long smoke-blackened deerskin shirt flapping almost to his knees.

Lea saw that the old man still had the Greener shotgun strapped on his back. Gunstock property, that piece, but the old man looked to have appropriated it.

Lea walked to a small ledge and looked east again, trying to see the riders. For a while, he saw nothing. That was bad news, because it could mean they were trying to come in secretly.

But why? Gunstock had nothing to do with him anymore. Not even if the Baron had died. There was no law to chase him for those dead drifters. Even if there were, they wouldn't be getting this fast a start after him.

Then he saw them—still a couple of miles out, still far down the hill.

Two men. Riding down a long meadow toward a stand of dwarf willow. A long way down the hill yet, but dead on his trail, and riding out in the open.

He heard hooves clattering behind him, and turned to look. Old Tocsen was riding up on his little paint pony, set to travel. It seemed that Lea had a trail pard, like it or not.

Tocsen kicked the paint up to the top of the knob, and sat the little pony beside Lea, watching the riders far below. Those two men seemed to be running their horses pretty hard. Moving up fast.

Tocsen sighed and farted. The old son-of-a-bitch had had the good sense to get his breakfast at the kitchens before he rode out of Gunstock. The old man was no fool, anyway you sliced it.

"Decide. We go—or we stay?"

"We stay," Lea said, before he knew he was going to say it. "We'll see what these two want."

Tocsen grunted, shook his head, and climbed down off the fat paint.

Lea walked over to the dun, and slid the Sharps out of the scabbard. He had a few of the big cartridges in his vest pockets, and he dug into his saddlebags for a few more. It might turn out to be a long day. Then he came back to the ledge, and hunkered down beside the old Indian. They would watch and wait and bask in the hot mountain sun. And in an hour or so, they'd climb down a little lower on the trail and find good places to greet the horsemen riding up.

Lea wished to God he had something to eat. His belly was kissing his backbone.

The riders made good time.

Leaving their horses reined over the knoll, Lea and Tocsen had worked a couple of hundred yards down the trail and picked their stands, Lea farther down, in a rock shadow a few steps to the side of the track; the Shoshone higher, in a tangle of fallen lodge-pole pine. Then the distant sounds, the scrape and clatter of driven horses on a stony trail, came echoing up the mountainside.

Lea stood well back into the shadow's coolness, the sleek weight of the Sharps balanced in his hand. At the bend in the track here, he could probably do as well, maybe even better, going for his first shot with the Colt, getting the Sharps into action if the second man took a run for it. He'd need the rifle in his hands for

75

that long shot.

So, it would be the Sharps, all the way.

Now, he could hear the creak of saddle leather. He took a quick look around—back up the trail, and higher on either side, up in the rocks. Once, some deputies in New Mexico had tracked him for a shooting, tracked him high. And they'd been smart enough to send their horses up a mountain trail, making all that noise, while they circled around afoot. It had almost worked.

He didn't see Tocsen when he looked back. He didn't expect to, though why the old man was putting his hat in this ring at all was a question.

Lea saw the horse's shadow come lunging across the trail from behind the sheer side of a huge yellow boulder. The mountain light was fiercely bright, like theatre limelight.

He knew the rider. A Gunstock cowhand named Folliard. An old man, almost sixty. A stringy, tough old man. What the hell he was chasing trail for?

Then the second horse and rider came out. The horse, a broad-chested sorrel, grunted as it took the fresh stony slope after the turn.

Another Gunstock cowpoke. Edwards . . . Edwins . . . some name like that.

They had no reason on earth to be trailing him. Both cowboys were armed. Spencers in their saddle boots, pistols stuck down into those clumsy holsters cowhands used. And something more, something Lea felt about them. Something he knew, just looking at them.

They weren't looking for trouble, and not fearing it. They had about them only the natural kind of alertness any man had better have in this country.

They were looking tired. Their horses were tired.

They'd come far and fast in a half day's riding. Coming after him.

He let Folliard ride up to within five yards of him. Then Lea took three strides and stepped out onto the trail in front of him, cocking the Sharps as he went.

Folliard's head snapped back in surprise, and he reined his horse hard so that it reared and tried to turn away. The old cowhand gentled it, his eyes on the muzzle of the Sharps.

"You scared the poop out of me, mister!"

Lea saw the second man draw up on the trail below. He wasn't reaching for a weapon. He stared up at Lea, hands still on his reins.

"You're on my track. You tell me why."

Lea saw the old man's adam's apple bounce.

"Hell, Mr. Lea, we're just doing like we was told!"

"Say what?"

"Budreau said Mister Bridge wanted you back at Gunstock—pronto. Said we was to ask you real friendly if you would come back, you know." He reached down carefully to pat his restive horse's neck, his eyes still on the Sharps. "We sure didn't mean to spook you. We was just sent with a message. That's all."

The other cowhand came up the trail to side his buddy. Lea now recognized him, name and all. Nat Edwinson, a bald man with a bad ear.

"And they sent you two riding this hard just to invite me back to the hotel. That's what you're saying?"

"That's it," old Folliard said. "Budreau said the old man was real anxious to see you back there."

"That's what he said," Nat Edwinson chimed in. His sorrel was sweating from the climb. "He comin', Bob?"

"Hell, I don't know," old Folliard said, and they sat

their shifting horses staring down at Lea with "We-done-our-job" expressions, waiting to see what he had to say.

"That German Baron dead, is he?"

"Him? Hell, no," Nat Edwinson said. "Not that I heard."

"No, he's all right. No trouble about that that I know about," Folliard said. "And I'd sure be obliged if you'd lower the muzzle on that there Sharps."

Lea looked at them both a moment more, then he lowered the rifle.

Folliard looked relieved. "I'm obliged," he said.

Lea stood for almost a full minute, thinking, ignoring the waiting cowhands. He had never found it a good idea to backtrail—especially if he'd had a damn good reason to leave in the first place. And Abe might be needing a neck to stretch—needing it bad—if the Baron had gone and died, and there'd been real trouble about it: like maybe some talk of murder by his own hunting guide.

"What else did Budreau say to you?" He gave Folliard a hard look as he asked it.

"Mr. Lea, that's all the man said, what I told you!" The old cowpoke seemed genuinely exasperated. "Mr. Bridge is real anxious to have you come back to see him; that's all I know!"

If the Baron was dead, he and Tocsen both could be in deep trouble with Abe Bridge. Still, lying and trapping just wasn't Abe's style. If Abe had wanted Lea hanged, the old man would have come after him himself to do it; and with a dozen men to give him a hand.

Still, a man *would* be a damn fool to backtrack into

trouble, just to satisfy his curiosity.

Lea heard horses on the trail above.

He turned fast, the Sharps coming up, and saw Tocsen riding down the track on his pony, leading Lea's big dun behind him.

While Lea'd been thinking about it, the old Indian had gone to get the horses for the ride back.

The Shoshone knew a damn fool when he saw one.

CHAPTER NINE

It was a long ride back. Too long for the tired horses.

They camped at dark in a fold of the hills, just seven miles out from Gunstock. It was a dry cold camp. The north wind was bringing the breath of winter into the mountains.

Lea and the cowhands sat at a small brushwood fire, blankets around their shoulders. Lea puffed at the last inch of a cigar while the cowpokes shifted their chaws, stared at the fire, and spit into the coals every now and then.

Tocsen sat across from them, wrapped in a very dirty old Hudson's Bay blanket. The Shoshone stared into the flames, his hooded eyes unwinking.

Lea'd never known much about old Tocsen. He'd known a lot of Indians, but he'd never been fool enough to think he understood them.

Folliard was telling the story of how he'd come west, when he was young, to go farming in Oregon. The ox-train had been wintered in, and he and two other young men had gone to work for a rancher in Colorado

—started in cowboying and never stopped.

The scrub fire slowly burned lower, falling in on itself in brittle bright-red coals. The night deepened around them until the stars crowded the black sky above them like clouds of silver dust. The wind blew stronger from the north.

Lea got up from the fire, stretched the stiffness out of his joints, then walked off into the dark, carrying the Sharps. He liked to sleep back from a fire in camp. It lessened the chances of an unpleasant surprise.

He found a small hollow in the hillside above the camp, maybe fifty yards up from the fire. There was tall grass there, matted, winter-killed, and soft enough. He laid the Sharps down and, wrapped in his blanket, lay down beside it, the brim of his gray Stetson tugged down to protect his face from the wind sighing down the steep hillside.

Tomorrow would likely be an interesting day.

They rode into Gunstock well before noon.

The Russian Count and his Cossacks had met them on the way, thundering by at a gallop, looking ready enough to run them off the road.

"There's a bunch I could learn to dislike real easy," Folliard said.

"That there's the man that whipped that horse," Nat Edwinson said. "He sure is big."

Lea turned in his saddle to see the last of the Cossacks disappearing around a bend in the trail. They rode well; there was no saying they didn't. Lea'd heard about that horse-whipping, and he'd heard, too, that Tiny Morgan, the huge half-witted stablehand, had gone wild with anger when he'd seen what had been done to the animal. Lea thought it probable that the Cossack, giant though he was, had been lucky Tiny Morgan hadn't been at the stable the day he lashed that horse half to death.

Seeing the Russians had brought Edna's wild tale to mind. The Count and old man Larrabee . . . a hidden fortune in silver ore.

"You stupid son-of-a-bitch!"

Abe Bridge sat glowering in his big leather swivel chair. Across the wide desk, Lea stood, looking back at the old man, not saying a word. It wasn't the first time Lea'd been called a son-of-a-bitch. Lea'd stopped killing men because of name-calling a lot of years ago.

The old man scowled furiously at him, his gray beard wagging to emphasize every word.

"Why in Christ's name didn't you just *explain* yourself?" He shook his head impatiently. "I know, I know . . . Sarah gave you a little tongue whippin', and told you to get out. But God in heaven, man, *I* run Gunstock. You could have come and told me what those owl-hooters tried to do!"

He muttered, and dug into a desk drawer for a folded sheet of paper, tattered and trailworn. He unfolded it, and slapped it down on the desk in front of Lea.

"Take a look at that, you fool. When the Baron told me what had happened, I sent some men out to the slash to bring those bodies in. The young one was carrying this."

Lea bent over the desk to look at it. A wanted poster —for three bank robbers. Thomas Deke, a man named Murrey, and a boy. No name for the boy.

"So, why the hell didn't you come and see me before

you high-tailed out of here? Tell me that!"

"I didn't want to get mixed up in this, for a lot of people to hear about, Mr. Bridge."

That was telling the old man straight.

And the old man took it straight.

Abe grunted and stared hard into Lea's eyes for a few moments, then reached out to pick up the wanted poster. He folded it, and stuffed it back into the cluttered desk drawer.

"I don't suppose we have to noise it around the country every time some high-grader gets out-gunned in the Bitteroots," he said. "The Baron's pleased enough with himself as it is." He leaned back in the big chair. "So, we'll let him play the hero. You just stand back and keep your mouth shut."

"The Baron's going to be all right?"

"Hell, yes. Or so Edwards says. He's up in his suite right now, telling every damn fool dude in the place how he shot it out with three hardcase outlaws. The fool's proud as punch!" Abe got up from behind his desk and went over to a big walnut humidor resting on a side table. "Cigar?"

"Thanks."

Abe walked over to Lea and handed him three of the big Havanas. "Take three," he said. "That's for saving that German's ass."

"He did some saving on his own. He made a fine rifle shot."

Abe grunted and went back behind his desk. "So I've heard—so everybody's heard!" He settled back into the big chair with a sigh. "Now, I presume you're back on the payroll. Will you please get your butt up to the penthouse suite? The Baron's been asking for you all morning. And when you're finished with that non-sense, there's a party due to go out for partridge after lunch. Take 'em, and show 'em some shootin'."

"Like this?"

Abe glanced at Lea's trail-blackened buckskins.

"Why not? The dudes expect a mountain man to smell like a horse. Now get on up there!"

Lea went up the back stairs. Abe or not, he didn't care to make an ass of himself by stomping up the grand staircase dirt-black and smoke-stained, with rifle in hand, so that the ladies coming down for the buffet lunch would have something to goggle at.

Abe was a good man. The best. He'd do his best to keep Lea's name out of the hoorah over the dead outlaws. But three dead men were three dead men. In all common sense Lea should be over the Bitteroots by now, not going up a dozen flights of stairs to be gawked at by the Baron's friends.

Two young maids came giggling down the service stairs past him, eying him as they went past with a swish of starched black skirts. They'd have heard all about it, of course. Back stairs knew front stairs, top to bottom. No secrets were kept.

Lea wondered where Edna was working. The little Irish girl would be glad to see him back.

He pushed through the heavy green door at the top of the stairs, and walked down the deeply carpeted corridor toward the penthouse. Gas lamps flickered behind their cut-glass shields on either side of the passage as he went—one of Abe's expensive luxuries. The little gas plant below the kitchen gardens had cost him a pretty penny—and stunk up the place when the wind was wrong.

Near the end of the corridor, a tall, paneled oak door stood ajar. Lea could hear laughter and the clink of glasses. The Baron must be feeling a damn sight better than he had in the slash timbers two evenings before.

Lea paused before the doorway, and rapped two or three times on the carved paneling. After a few moments, the door swung open, and the Baron's man, Otto, stood looking up at Lea, with a cold, faintly surprised expression on his face.

"Yes?" Otto said. He was a short, dumpy little German, with a complexion white as a corpse's. He was dressed like a corpse, too, in a neat black suit and shiny black shoes.

"Farris Lea. The Baron's expecting me."

Otto seemed to doubt it. "I don't believe—"

"Oh, get out of my way!" Lea walked through the little man, ignored his clucks and gobbles, leaned the long Sharps against the entrance hallway's velvet-covered wall, and strode on into the suite's sitting room.

A dozen people were there, gathered around the long sofa under the windows. Sunlight was streaming in, filling the room with tiger-stripes of sun and shadow. The Baron, looking pale and tired, but cheerful enough, lay propped against a pile of pillows, wrapped in a long, quilted green silk dressing gown.

They turned to look at Lea as he walked into the room.

A few of the really rich dudes were there: Señor Bibao, the Marquis of Stene, and old man Larrabee—pink, short, round and fat, with his snowy mutton-chops, looking like old Santa Claus himself. And others: Leo Drexel and Toby Easterby, and Dr. Edwards. The

Baron's sister was there, too, sitting by the sofa with a needlework sampler on her lap. Erica, her name was. A handsome woman, tall and thin. Pretty, too, with those pale, pale eyes and ash-blonde hair, almost white.

Sarah Bridge was standing by the window, looking out over the sweep of the drive to the carriage road and the mountains beyond. When Lea walked in, she turned from the window to look at him. A flash of anger showed in those blue eyes. Not too happy to see Farris Lea back again. Not after she'd ordered him off.

Lea smiled at her as if butter wouldn't melt in his mouth.

"Ah, dere he iss—my fateful guide!" The Baron's English was off a bit this morning. The burly German sat up on the sofa, holding his hand out for Lea to shake. It looked as though the Baron wanted some kind of theatrics, so Lea sighed and obliged, striding over to the sofa like any rough-but-honest mountain man, and giving the Baron's big paw a firm and manly pumping.

"What a fellow dis iss!" the Baron said, letting go of Lea's hand. "Between us, we killed dos tree quick!"

"Bravo," said the Marquis of Stene. He was sitting across the room in a chair by the fireplace, and didn't seem very impressed by the theatrics. But young Toby Easterby said, "Damn well done!" and seemed to mean it. "I just wish I'd been there, that's all."

"Well," Lea said, "old Tocsen did us some good out there."

"Modest," said the Marquis, and yawned.

"Yes," old man Larrabee said, and he nodded at Lea from across a coffee table loaded with cake and cinnamon rolls. "Yes," the old man said, nodding and smiling like Santa Claus, "good man, good man."

Lea thought for a moment Larrabee was going to offer him a cup of coffee. But no such luck. The frontiersman was here on exhibit, not as a guest. He felt a sudden hot anger against these people, these damn stupid snobs who didn't know or care who the hell they were talking to. What would they say if he told them "I'm Buckskin Frank Leslie. I've killed more than forty men, face to face, gun to gun. From Anchorage to Vera Cruz men fear my name. I've lived high in New York City, Chicago, San Franciso and Montreal. I've loved Jenny Lind, and spent one night with Lilly Langtry."

"Mr. Lea has done just what he was hired to do," said Sarah Bridge from the window. "No more, and no less."

CHAPTER TEN

Coming down from the Baron's suite, Lea took the grand staircase. He didn't give a damn what the guests thought. He came fast down the center of the wide, carpeted stairs, furious and scowling, the big buffalo gun swinging in his hand. The guests using the staircase looked up in surprise and quickly stepped aside. Except one. Count Yuri Orloff stood waiting at the bottom of the stairs.

The Count's riding clothes and high boots were mud-spattered from his gallop. Still, standing on the thick Turkish carpet, its blaze of greens and reds and patterned gold a backdrop for his slender, elegant figure, he seemed as much at home as he had thundering at the head of his band of Cossacks.

The Count smiled as Lea walked frowning down to him.

"You seem to be out of temper, hunter," he said. "Perhaps an overdose of civilization."

Lea said nothing, and would have walked on by, but the Russian reached out one small white hand, and held his arm.

They both stood still for a moment at the foot of the staircase. At the touch of the count's hand, Lea had turned to face him, his gray eyes as cold and dark as ocean ice.

For just a moment, the Russian's black eyes widened, then narrowed like a cat's when faced with sudden danger. Then he laughed.

"Yes. I think an overdose of civilization."

"Count," Lea said, "take your hand off my arm."

"Of course," Orloff said, and his hand dropped to his side as he bowed. "You must forgive me, Mr. Lea. I have become used to dealing with *softer* types of Americans." He smiled. "I'd forgotten that some of you frontiersmen are very like our Siberian hunters . . . and bandits." His smile didn't waver. "So very touchy—so proud."

Lea felt a sudden urge to hit the man, to knock that smile off his face. He had a quick vision of the small Russian lying across the stairs, snarling, bloody mouthed.

"What do you want, Count Orloff?"

"Why, only a little grouse shooting, Mr. Lea. What else should I want?" Of course. Old Abe had told him: a party to take out. The Russian stood watching him, smiling.

"All right. We'll go up the hill north of the drive. There're grouse up there about a mile and half. There's a stand of young pine they like. We'll take a spaniel up there to flush them."

"One of my men will come to carry my guns . . . if you don't mind, Mr. Lea?"

"I don't mind, Count," Lea said. He'd heard the

89

Count liked to have one of his Cossacks along when he went out with a gun. Probably needed a bodyguard where he came from.

Lea met them at the east end of the terrace, half an hour later.

The Count had changed to canvas trousers and a shooting jacket, and he wore them as elegantly as if he were going to dinner with the Czar. The Cossack standing behind him wasn't so neat. Lea had seen men like him all over the West, and this Russian model wasn't much different. Big, in a neat black uniform with bright brass buttons. Big, with a face that looked hacked out of oak. A pair of muddy, slanted brown eyes, a big beak of a nose, a long, dropping mustache over a slash of mouth.

A killer—a disciplined one. Lea had known cavalry NCO's like this; big, brutal Irishmen and blacks. Men treated cruelly by life, held under ferocious discipline —ready to repay cruelty with cruelty.

"This is Josef," the Count said, gesturing to the Cossack standing behind him.

"This is Pee-wee," said Lea in the same tone of voice. The springer spaniel yelped with pleasure at the sound of its name, and frisked around Lea's feet, anxious to get hunting.

"Well," the Count said, and he bent to pet the excited dog. "Shall we be going?"

"I say! I say, you chaps!"

Lea turned, and saw Toby Easterby trotting across the terrace toward them. He was wearing the odd outfit that English people seemed to think appropriate for bird shooting: a checked tweed suit, high brown shoes, and a strange fore-and-aft-hat. A deer-stalker hat, was what they called it. You couldn't tell if it was coming or going.

"I say . . . do you chaps mind, I mean would you mind awfully if I went along?" He had a nice-looking 20-gauge double, a Purdy, Lea thought, broken across his arm.

"I mean, I don't want to be *de trop,* you know, if you fellows would rather go out alone."

"Oh, I think you're welcome enough, Mr. Easterby," Lea said. He'd hunted with the young Englishman before, and funny hat or not, the boy could shoot a scattergun.

"You don't mind, Count?" Easterby said.

"Certainly not . . ." The Count bowed. "Your company will be the greatest pleasure to us . . ."

Still, from the hard glitter in the Russian's narrow black eyes, Lea thought he'd as soon not have Toby Easterby along. He was angry about something—probably afraid the Englishman'd show him up on the grouse. Fast, difficult targets, grouse.

Lea leashed in the spaniel and moved out across the drive, up the hill. Pee-wee was the apple of the Gunstock kennelman's eye, a big liver-and-white dog, friendly as a pup, and a terror around birds. "A range like a pointer's, and a setter's flush," the kennelman said. He was pretty much right. Pee-wee (named as the runt of the litter, before he began to fill out) was a dandy bird dog. Old Abe had gotten some very handsome offers for Pee-wee; had refused every one. He'd made some good friends for Gunstock by breeding the big dog to prime bitches and then sending the pups out as presents to the grander sportsmen among

Gunstock's regular guests.

As it turned out, Count Orloff had no reason to fear comparison with Easterby's shooting. The Russian was a superb shot, one of the best men with a shotgun that Lea had ever seen. Even a better shot than Lea with a scattergun.

The Russian had made a few shots that Lea would have thought impossible. One of them, a crossed double against two grouse flying like bullets in opposite directions. It was a double kill that left Toby Easterby groaning in disbelief.

"Good God! Orloff, you just ain't human!"

The Count had smiled and passed his gun back to the Cossack for reloading.

"A lucky day for me, I think," he said.

"Luck ain't in it." Easterby said. "Is it, Lea?"

"No," Lea said, "it isn't luck. It's the best passing shooting I ever saw."

The Count didn't answer, because Pee-wee, knowing a hot gun when he hunted with one, had already charged into a fresh bank of pine scrub, his stub of a tail spinning with joy as he ran.

The Cossack handed the loaded gun back to his master, and the Count hefted the gleaming piece, watching the dog, waiting for the birds to explode out of the tangle of green.

They came fast, whirring out of the pines in a drum of wing beats, weaving through the air grass high.

Then the Count stood back, smiling, letting Easterby take his shot.

The young Englishman, unnerved by the Russian's shooting, took his first shot and his second—and missed both times.

One grouse settled. The other two were gone, at least

eighty yards out and traveling fast.

The Count stepped up, snapped the shotgun's stock to his shoulder, and killed both birds.

"Have you ever seen shooting to equal that?" Toby Easterby asked Lea as they walked toward the kennels to return Pee-wee. The Count and his Cossack had gone straight back to the hotel.

Lea whistled Pee-wee to heel, and shifted the seven brace of grouse, tied by their feet to a loop of cord, to his other hand. The kitchen would be glad to get them.

"Not with a shotgun," he said. "With that, I think he's the best I ever saw."

"Good lord, I wonder if the fellow's as fine a shot with a revolver and a rifle."

"No," Lea said. "He wouldn't be. He might be a *good* shot with a pistol or a rifle. But not the way he is with a shotgun. Each weapon takes a different hand and eye . . ."

"Well, thank heavens for that. The fellow would be insupportable!"

Lea didn't say anything. Whatever he might think about the Count, he'd learned to steer clear of the guests' quarrels.

"Fellow's always smiling, don't you know . . . as if he knew a jolly good joke, and the joke was on you."

Young Easterby left Lea at the south terrace, and went off to change. Chef de la Maine was glad enough to see the grouse when Lea took them into the kitchen.

"We can use these . . . yes," he said. "We hang them a little while . . . then we shall see." He felt the little bird breasts. "I think a pie . . ."

Lea left the kitchen and went looking for Edna. The Irish girl must have heard he'd come back that morning. Lea'd expected to see her waiting for him in

93

the kitchen—or, if de la Maine was in a bad mood, in the servant's dining room. No luck. A girl name Sally Connell was in the dining room drinking coffee and making cow's eyes at a groom. Sykes was the groom's name; he was a tough, thin mountaineer from Tennessee.

"Sally," Lea said, "you seen Edna?"

"No, I haven't, Mr. Lea."

Sykes shook his head too. They both stared at Lea, thinking, probably, about the gunfight at the slash.

"Well, when you do see her, tell her I was asking."

They both nodded, still staring. It annoyed Lea; the Baron was supposed to be the big shooter. He didn't blame the girl for looking bug-eyed, but Sykes should have known better than to goggle.

You could never tell about women. He'd been sure Edna would be damn glad to see him back again.

It would be like the little bitch to give him the go-bye, and then to show up in his cabin as a surprise. Lea hesitated, then walked across the cobbled yard to the stables. He owed that old dun a lot.

Tiny Morgan was there, mucking out the mares' stalls, and doing the work of at least two men, judging by the pile of straw and manure heaped by the stable door. He looked up as Lea walked in, and smiled the wide, innocent smile of a child.

"Good afternoon, Mister Lea," he said. It had taken Tiny some effort to learn the difference between morning, afternoon, and evening. But once he'd done it, he found that he liked the *sound* of afternoon best. So it was afternoon, as far as Tiny was concerned, from dawn to dusk.

"Afternoon, Tiny. How's the dun doing?"

"Oh, fine, fine!" Tiny spread his massive arms to show how well, how big and fine the dun was feeling.

"He's been eatin' some mash."

Lea took a look at the dun himself, just to be sure. But Tiny had done his job well. The big horse looked rested and at ease. A few hard rides were in the old boy yet.

When he left the dun, Lea saw that Tiny was again cleaning out the mares' stalls.

"Say, Tiny!" he called. "Have you seen Miss Edna today?"

Edna was a favorite of Tiny's, because she sometimes brought him candy left over from children's parties at the hotel. A surprising number of Gunstock's guests were willing to bring their children out to the wilderness, as long as they never left the hotel grounds.

Tiny liked Edna for another reason, too. She was one of the few Irish girls who weren't frightened of the big halfwit.

"Oh, Miss Edna was here early in the afternoon." Lea knew he meant morning. "Then she went away."

Lea walked back toward his cabin. If she wasn't there, then to hell with her. He'd go to the wash-shed and buy a hot bath from Bobby Chen. God knows he needed one.

He lifted the latch on the cabin door, and eased the door open slowly, braced for the girl's rush—or a pail of water on his head! Edna, drunk, had once braced a pail of water over his door for forgetting her birthday.

Lea eased the door open, then suddenly shoved it wider and jumped inside.

A knife came out of the dark and struck him over the heart.

CHAPTER ELEVEN

Lea felt the impact, the bright, slicing pain. He knew it was a knife. And he knew he might be dead in less than half a minute.

He kicked out hard and hit something. He leaped from the doorway deeper into the cabin's shadowy darkness, then doubled into a somersault over the rough pine floor, drawing the slim Arkansas toothpick from his right boot as he came to his feet. He was alive.

He cursed the civilized manners of Gunstock. He hadn't worn his .45 to go out bird-shooting with the Russian count.

Lea stood in the close darkness, not breathing, not moving.

The man with the knife had been careful; the wooden shutter had been shut over the little cabin's one window. It was as dark as a closet in the small room.

Lea felt the warm blood running down his chest under the slashed buckskin shirt. There was no way to tell how bad it might be. The jump he'd made into the cabin had thrown the knifeman off. Lea had taken the edge instead of the point.

Lea breathed softly through his open mouth, listening.

He felt it before he heard it: the sudden warm draft of air at his back.

Lea spun, crouching low, and thrust up hard with the needle-pointed toothpick.

The knife bucked in his hand. He heard a sharp cry of surprise as the double-edged blade slid home. Lea was hit in a furious driving charge that straightened him up and slammed him across the dark room and into the opposite wall with a crash. Only a strong man would have the strength to do that.

Lea spun away from the wall, stepping into the darkness. The man drove in again.

Lea jumped back to the wall, letting his boots sound loud, and spun away again. As the man came in again, going for the sound like a bear, Lea whirled back to the wall and swung the toothpick, wanting nothing more than to nail the son-of-a-bitch to the wall.

He felt the long blade slide into meat—and into the logs beneath it.

The man bellowed and struck out with his own blade. Lea heard it slice the air over his head.

Lea's wrist was almost sprained as the man tore free.

The bastard was as strong as an ox.

No doubt about it—it was Budreau. The sweet stink of macassar oil hung in the cabin's close air.

The burly ranch foreman had waited with his big hook-bladed Bowie.

Lea'd gotten steel into Budreau twice. But the big foreman didn't seem weaker—or slower. Budreau was a professional with a knife. Lea had thought so when he'd first seen the bow-legged foreman swaggering around Gunstock, the big Bowie sheathed at his hip.

Lea didn't like the odds. He could fight with a knife, and had killed men with them, but Budreau was an expert. The cabin was dark, and Lea's home territory, otherwise Lea's guts would already be warming the floor. That fast move at the door had given Lea a break.

Budreau came at him once again. Lea caught just a glimpse of him in the shadowy light, a darker darkness moving in.

Lea moved left, then jumped out to the right. He knew it was a mistake while he was still in the air.

An instant later Lea felt the steel slice his side, graze a rib, and cut free.

Lea struck back with the toothpick, and missed. Budreau was gone, back into the dark.

Lea felt the blood pouring from his side. His whole side was burning, searing in agony. It was hard to breathe.

The next time Budreau might kill him.

Lea began edging his way along the cabin's short back wall. He tried to stifle his gasps as he breathed; he was starting to feel sick to his stomach. He could hear the soft sounds of blood dripping onto the pine floor. Budreau laughed, a soft chuckle from across the dark cabin.

He was cut up himself, maybe cut bad. Yet he laughed, laughed at the hoarse breathing, the stumbling shuffle along the wall, the dripping sounds.

Lea leaned against the wall, slid along it a step at a time. He listened for Budreau. The big man had stopped chuckling. There was no sound in the dark, no sound at all, except for his own labored breathing, the scrape and shuffle of his boots along the cabin floor.

He heard the pine creak.

The knifeman was coming.

Lea fumbled with his weapon, got the grip he wanted, and felt along the wall in front of him. The floor boards creaked again, nearer.

Lea braced his legs and reached over the cabin's window sill. He felt in the darkness, then found the shutter.

Sunlight flooded the cabin in a rush of gold and Lea saw Budreau standing frozen ten feet away, blotches of red where the toothpick had bitten him. Lea spun, whipped his arm back, and threw his knife overhand with all the strength he had.

The big man blinked in the blaze of light, saw the blade flashing toward him, and, as light on his feet as a girl, swayed out to the right to let it pass.

He moved right into it.

Lea had learned long ago that right-handed men tended to duck to the right.

The toothpick slid into Budreau's throat, the slim double-edged blade buried deep.

For an instant, the big man stood stock still, his face contorted in shock, glaring down at the knife-grip thrusting out from under his chin.

He convulsed, clawing at the dagger, staggering across the cabin's sunlit floor, spitting and gargling as he tried to breathe.

Rather than watch the man, Lea watched the knife. Gleaming, with just the slightest smear of blood across the shimmering steel, the big knife fell to the white pine floor as its master stumbled, drowning in his own blood.

Finally, Budreau lay down. He sat first, red with blood. He managed then to pull the toothpick from his throat. He sat holding it in his hand for a moment, then fell onto his side, trying to die.

Lea had had enough. He limped over to the cold stove, picked up a piece of firewood from beside it, and smashed in Budreau's head.

Otto had served the Baron ever since the death of the old Baron. The old Baron had taken Otto out of the stables and made a servant of him. Otto never knew why he'd been so favored, but he'd been grateful, and faithful, in return.

No man could say that the present Baron was in any way as good a man as his father had been.

"Take care of my boy, Otto," the old man had said.

Otto had taken care of the young Baron. Very good care, indeed.

Still, he was not really prepared to deal with this howling wilderness, filled with savages and madmen. Idaho was worse than Italy! And that was saying a great deal.

It was not enough that his master lay wounded, not by a French bullet in an honorable war, but shot in the woods by horse thieves!

And now, not yet content, the Baron must send him to this hunting guide's shack. And with a bottle of champagne! A gift for the fellow!

And what for, God alone knew. It was, after all, the Baron who had done what fighting needed to be done against those three ruffians.

Otto marched up to the cabin door carrying the

bottle of champagne in a silver bucket filled with cracked ice. It had taken him a while to find it in the maze of stables, shacks, bunkhouses and storage bins behind the main building of the huge hotel.

Otto knocked. There was no answer.

He knocked again, tapping his foot impatiently on the cabin's door-sill.

He reached out to knock once more. It was likely that this specimen of frontier trash had gone off to the hotel kitchens to eat and get drunk with his fellow servants.

But, as he knocked, Otto heard a sound inside. The fellow was home.

There was another sound behind the cabin door. The latch was lifted, and the door slowly swung open.

Then, standing right in front of him in the doorway, was the most appalling sight that Otto had ever seen. It was a man *covered* in blood, with a stick of wood—a club—in his hand.

As Otto stood, staring at this horror, the bloody man said something, swayed, and fell into his arms.

"Oh, heavens, heavens! What am I to tell *Herr Baron?*"

"Really, Otto, the Baron is hardly likely to care about a dropped bottle of champagne in these circumstances!"

"But it was *Perrier-Jouet!* The Baron chose it himself for a gift!"

Lea thought he was dreaming. An uncomfortable dream. His side hurt like hell.

He thought old Abe's snotty daughter was looking down at him. She looked sorry for him. "Oh, where is that damn doctor!" She didn't sound very ladylike.

101

"Hold on, Mister Lea—just hold on! The doctor is coming." She looked as though she were about to cry.

"Don't cry," Lea said. He knew it was no dream. He remembered it all. But for Christ's sake, the girl was looking at him as if he were dying!

Lea said to her as clearly as he could, "Listen, I'm just cut up a little. I'll be fine. Don't cry."

It must have been the wrong thing to say, because she started crying in earnest. He thought, maybe, that he was dreaming after all.

He woke hurting as much as he had hurt in a long time.

He was in a room in the hotel, he could see that, but it was night. The room's curtains were drawn and just over the foot of the bed, he saw a fire burning behind the isinglass of a Franklin stove. Old Abe's daughter was sitting on the other side of the bed, looking at him.

"Are you in pain, Mr. Lea?" She wasn't a beauty, but she did have nice blue eyes. "Mr. Lea. Are you in pain?"

"A little," Lea croaked, cleared his throat and tried again. "Just a little . . . my side."

"Yes. Your side was the worst. The wound on your chest was not quite so bad . . ." She got up from her chair, went to a basin beside the head of the bed, dipped a cloth in water, and wrung it out. "It is very late at night, Mr. Lea. Your . . . your fight took place this afternoon." She folded the cloth and reached down to put it across his forehead. It felt cool and good.

"How bad are the cuts?"

She pursed her lips. "Bad enough. But the doctor said they should heal fairly quickly."

"Not fast enough to make any difference!" It was Old Abe's voice. And it sounded cold as ice.

102

The old man walked into the room, and left the door open behind him. "Sarah, you get on out of here, now."

"Father, he needs someone to nurse him."

"No, he doesn't." Abe stood at the bedside, looking down into Lea's face. "I'm hanging the son-of-a-bitch in the morning."

CHAPTER TWELVE

Lea didn't think for a minute the old man was joking.

His daughter didn't either. Lea saw Sarah Bridge's face grow pale. The year before Lea had come from Montana to Gunstock, four drifters had come riding by the great hotel and its cattle ranch, and asked for a handout. They'd gotten a few day's lodging, food, and fodder for their horses. Then they'd ridden out.

They'd paused in the high pastures, long enough to steal forty head of beef.

Abe and his ranch hands were after them the next day. They caught them, too, just the other side of High Pass. Abe hanged all four in the lodge-pole pines.

No, Lea didn't think the old man was joking.

He tried to move in the soft hotel bed, but a streak of pain ran up his side that took his breath away. He glanced at the bedside table—no gun. The old man had him cold.

"Father—"

"You get out of this room right now, Sarah!"

"But—"

"Damn you, girl! Did you hear me? I said clear out of this room—*pronto!*"

Nobody argued with Abe Bridge when he looked like that.

Sarah, her face white with anger, turned without a word and went out.

When she was gone Abe stood glaring down at him. Lea hitched himself up onto his elbow. He didn't figure he had much to lose.

"What's all this talk about hanging, Abe? That pig Budreau laid for me in my own place, and attacked me!"

"Yes. And why would he do that, Lea? Except if he found out, and came to get you for it!" The old man looked ready to hit him.

Lea felt a cold, sick feeling in his guts.

"Get me? For what?"

The old man's fists were clenched, trembling.

"For choking the life out of that little girl . . . *that's* what."

"Edna?"

"As if you didn't know—you dirty son of a bitch!" Abe exploded. He reached down and caught Lea by the throat, and shook him; the strong, gnarled old miner's hands squeezing.

Lea twisted on the bed, his side, his chest in a flame of agony—clawing, trying to tear the old man's hands off his throat. The firelight was going, dimming, wavering as he fought. He saw only Abe Bridge's snarling face, shifting and rippling as if it were under dark water.

"You could have killed him!"

105

"By God, I *meant* to kill the son-of-a-bitch!"

"Get out of my way, both of you." The doctor's face swam out of the dark above Lea. He felt hands on his throat, the bandages at his side.

"Not bleeding again . . . no thanks to you, Mr. Bridge."

Lea forced his eyes open. The lids seemed very heavy. He saw the doctor bending over him, Sarah Bridge and old Abe standing just behind him.

"Welcome back, Lea," Dr. Edwards smiled down at him. "You've had quite a day!"

"And his last!" Abe Bridge said.

"What do you mean by that?" the doctor said.

"I mean he murdered that poor little Irish girl! That's what I mean by that!"

"The hell he did. Wasn't he riding back here with your own men last night?"

"That's right, doctor."

Edwards straightened the twisted bedsheet, folded it down, and examined the bandage over the cut on Lea's chest. "Mr. Bridge," he said, "that girl was strangled last night—and early in the night, at that."

"Then he couldn't have killed her," Sarah said, giving her father a very cold look.

"Not if he was on the trail with those ranchhands, riding in." Edwards pulled the sheet up over Lea's bandaged chest.

"I was—" Lea croaked, cleared his throat, and tried again. "I was with those men. Who found her?"

Abe pushed the doctor aside. "Listen, boy, I made a fool of myself here."

"Looks like . . ." said Sarah Bridge.

Abe glared at her. "Well, damnit, I'm responsible for

106

those girls! You think I'm going to let some dirty dog choke the life out of a little girl at Gunstock—and get away with it?" He reached down and took Lea's hand. "I'm sorry I flew off the handle, there, boy, but I knew damn well you'd been stepping out with that O'Malley girl. And, well . . ."

"Stepping out . . ?" said Sarah Bridge. This time it was Lea who got the cold look.

"Forget it," Lea croaked. "I understand . . ."

"Very handsome," Doctor Edwards said. "Now if the courtesies are over with, I'd like Mr. Lea to get some sleep. In fact, I insist on it."

"All right." Abe let Sarah lead him to the door. "I suppose it was Budreau."

Edwards looked down at Lea. "You must be in considerable pain, Mr. Lea."

"Not much."

"Ummm. Not much, you say?" He turned away to the bedside table and dug into his leather bag. "Well, I think we'll prescribe a few drops of laudanum all the same."

Lea spent the next three days and nights dreaming while awake. Edward's laudanum floated him down a river that flowed past everyone he'd known for many years. People who had died. People who had left him. Doc Holliday came walking into his dream, looking just as Lea had first seen him, in Fort Smith those many years ago.

"Frank Leslie," Doc had said, "I understand that you are a rare pisser indeed with a Colt. Is that so?" His bony, wasted, ugly little face was screwed up in curiosity. Lea thought the little dentist might be looking

107

for a fight.

"I cannot tell a lie," he said to the little man, smiling. "I am indeed a considerable hand with a six-gun."

"It's a lonely life, isn't it?" Holliday said to him, peering at Lea with those watery, pale blue eyes.

"Lonely, and bitter, and foolish," Lea had said to him.

Doc had laughed and nodded. He even bought the first round of beers. The other men in the bar had been disappointed. The silence had dissolved into murmurs, then laughter, as they all went back to their drinks and their games and their girls.

"You've dreamed of me enough, Frank," Doc said to Lea. "Remember me dying in Denver? You surely don't want to dream about that." Lea saw Holliday's small, bony hand clenched around the glass of beer. The beer was cold; the glass had frost on it. They'd brought snow down from the mountains to the Denver bars.

Lea awoke, thirsty, and knew he was awake. It was bright, cold, and sunny outside.

He thought at first there was nobody else in the room, then he saw old Tocsen squatting on his haunches in the sunlight under one of the tall windows. The old man was leaning back against the wall, smoking a sloppily rolled cigarette. Lea could smell the Bull Durham. The old Shoshone turned his head to look at Lea, as if he'd expected him to be awake at just that moment.

"You want water?" he said. "You want eat?"

"Water," Lea said, and watched the old man rise to his feet and shuffle over to the nightstand. Tocsen picked up the glass from the tray and dipped it into the water pitcher. He brought it up half full. Lea rolled up onto his elbow, feeling the dull, ache in his side as he did. He reached out, took the glass, and drank. He finished it in seconds.

"Want more?"

Lea shook his head and lay back down on the pillow. He didn't feel so bad. He didn't feel sick either. Just tired. Tired right down to his bones.

Old Tocsen took back the glass and stood beside the bed, staring down at him. He didn't seem too interested.

"Women come back by and by," he said to Lea. "By and by" was a phrase the old Shoshone was fond of.

"What women?" Lea said. He was asleep before the old man could answer him.

He dreamed he was standing on the bank of Rifle River, watering the dun. The dun was young again; his hide flashed sleek in the summer sunlight. He was mouthing the water, sucking it up in great gulps.

Lea dreamed he pulled the horse away, mounted him, and rode off into the meadows. He rode a long way, which passed quickly in the dream, and came to the west ridge that rose above the ranch.

There, he reined in the dun. He didn't want to ride over the crest for fear of what he'd see. The ranch all ruined and gone, maybe. Or buned out. Or never there at all.

Then he took a deep breath and spurred the big horse through the pines, up to the crest of the ridge.

It was there.

The big cabin with its square logs, the corral and sheds and stables. And the horses. He could see the appaloosas in the high pastures, the little colts and fillies trotting after the mares, the big stud higher on the hill.

The place looked good. He was glad he'd gone up to the crest of the ridge. Now he could see it all, all the broad pastures deep in grass, green with spring. The fields, the stands of hardwood and pine, the valley stretching out below.

He saw old Bupp come walking out of the stable. The old man was lugging grain buckets out to the corral. He seemed a little more stooped than usual.

Lea wondered if the Blackfoot was around. He'd be a fully grown man by now.

Then he saw the girl. She came riding out of the trees below the cabin, across the meadow on a little dapple mare. She had on a pair of trousers and a bright red calico shirt; a floppy-brimmed straw hat sat on her head. She was leading a pack-horse hitched up with sacks and boxes from town. Looked like she knew her business.

"Good girl," Lea said to her.

He stood up in his stirrups and called down to her. "Good girl!"

But he called too loud and felt himself spinning.

He could just see the mountains looming over the valley, their peaks sparkling with spring snowfall through the distance. The girl looked tiny. He thought she turned her face up to look at him.

When he woke again it was night. Sarah Bridge was sitting in the upholstered rocker by the bed, knitting something; it looked like an afghan, black, green, and gold. She was rocking a little, her soft brown hair shining in the lamplight. Lea lay still, watching her.

When she finally looked up from her work, she seemed a little startled to find him looking at her. "You're awake, Mr. Lea."

"Yes."

"Are you in pain?" She put aside her work and came to stand beside the bed.

"No." And he wasn't. The sharp ache along his side was gone. He felt stiff, awkward, all along his body.

"You've been very ill, Mr. Lea." She was mixing some brown medicine into the water glass.

"How long?"

"Three days," she said. "Here, please drink this."

"What is it?"

"Just an iron tonic. Nothing to be afraid of." She smiled at him. "I don't think it even tastes very bad."

It seemed to Lea that there was more to Sarah Bridge than he had thought. She appeared to have been nursing him, even though she'd never much liked him. She had beautiful blue eyes. The tonic tasted terrible.

CHAPTER THIRTEEN

He woke again just before dawn.

It was still dark outside the tall windows, but the darkness had a touch of gray, a soft light to it.

Lea turned his head on the pillow to take a quiet look at Sarah Bridge. She wasn't there.

Another woman, older, slim, dressed in gray, with pale ash-blonde hair was rocking slowly in the big rocking chair, reading a book.

It was the Baron's sister, Erica. What in blue hell was she playing nurse for? As far as Lea could remember, the Baron's sister had been even more of a snob than the Baron himself. People waited on her, not the other way around.

The German woman turned a page, then looked up to see Lea watching her. She stared back at him for a moment, her pale gray eyes expressionless. Then she smiled.

"Good morning, Herr Lea." She looked down at a little gold watch pinned to the bosom of her dress. "It is just now five o'clock."

"Good morning." Lea reached out for the water on the bedside table.

"No, no." She was out of the chair. "That is my task, as your nurse. Is it not?" She reached down to put an arm behind his shoulders, lifting him as she held the glass to his lips. She was stronger than she looked.

"Since you have been so brave in helping my dear brother against those bandits—" "I thought the least I could do was to relieve Miss Bridge. The poor child was quite exhausted." She put the glass down and plumped up the pillows behind him.

Lea felt one slender hand gently stroke the back of his neck. Then she arranged her wide silken skirt and sat carefully on the side of the bed, smiling at him.

"It doesn't hurt you if I do this?"

"No," Lea said. "I'm healed up pretty well." It was strange; the Baron's snotty sister had never struck him as the ministering-angel type.

"Yes, I think you are," the German woman said. She stared at Lea, the pale eyes still. She touched her lips with the tip of her tongue. "But a bad injury, the doctor said, especially the cut along your side." A flush of color rose in her white cheeks. "To have fought in such a way. To have fought in the darkness with knives, against a brute such as that! To have cut him like that, to have stabbed him and killed him!" She flushed again, and looked down at the carpet. "It was very brave."

"Not much," Lea said. "I was plenty scared."

She looked up at him, staring with those pale, pale eyes. "I don't think so," she said. "I think you like to fight, Mr. Lea. I think you enjoy the struggle when a man pits his strength against yours, attacks you with a weapon so you must kill him or be killed yourself."

113

"The hell I do," Lea said.

But the German woman just smiled, sitting on the edge of the bed, staring into his eyes. It was as if she knew something about him.

"I have known men like you," she said softly. "Men who kill people." The pink tip of her tongue showed again, touching her lips.

"I don't make a habit of it, lady," Lea said coldly. What the hell was this bitch after?

"No?" She smiled and stood up beside the bed, smoothing the wrinkles from her long skirt. "Don't you?"

She stood, looking down at him for a moment. In the dull gold of the lamplight, he could still see a small blue vein throbbing along the slim white column of her throat.

She cleared her throat. "I think that I had better change the bandage for you. It will be one less thing to be done by Miss Bridge in the morning."

"It feels all right," Lea said. "No need to bother."

"It is not a *bother*, Mr. Lea, it is something that must be done. Please to turn over onto your other side." She reached for the bandages and scissors on the bedside table.

Lea turned over onto his right side, half expecting a twinge of pain. There was none. Just a feeling of tightness, the scratchy discomfort of a row of stitches. A few days in bed and hours of sleep had fixed him up pretty damn well.

The sheet was pulled down from his shoulder, and in a moment he felt the German woman's cool hand resting against the muscles of his back.

He didn't even have a nightshirt on, but the lady

didn't seem to give a damn. He felt her cool fingers stroke for a moment along his back, then gently begin to work at the sticking plaster at the edges of the long bandage.

There was no doubt about it; the Baron's sister was enjoying herself. Lea had known women who liked a little violence in their lives. Most like violence at a safe distance, but there'd been one or two who liked it right in their lap. Jane Canary, for one. And that Mexican girl in Monterey. But near or far, the Baron's cold, thin sister had some interest in killing. Maybe it was in her blood. Lea remembered the Baron's eyes as he'd watched the three drifters riding away when they'd first sent them out of camp. A hard bunch, the Prussians.

"This will hurt you a little, I think."

Lea felt the cool fingers tugging at the tape holding the bandage along his side. He felt them grip and tear the whole bandage free.

"Damn it!"

"I said it would hurt you." The damn woman was laughing at him! "But not too badly I hope." The cool fingers were on him again, caressing.

"It is a terrible scar . . . ugly . . . red."

The hands were not so cool now. Lea winced as a fingertip prodded at the barely healed wound, and slowly traced the long scar down along his ribs.

"And you have other scars—here." The slim hand rested warm against his side. "You have fought men before, and killed them, haven't you, Mr. Lea?" Her voice was hoarse with pleasure.

Lea knew what she wanted.

"Yes. I've killed men."

Again, he felt her fingers trace the long, inflamed

115

scar, the ladder of stitches. She swallowed. "How have you . . . done it?"

He wanted to see her. He started to turn, but her hand was at his shoulder, stopping him.

"Tell me," she said. "Just tell me." Both her hands were on him then, rubbing gently up along the wound, fingertips feathers along the scar. Her slim hands felt hot.

"I've shot them," Lea said. His own voice was hoarse now, his throat tight. As her hands worked on him, rubbing harder, digging into the muscles of his side, he felt his cock stir against the smooth sheet. However the bitch wanted it; that's how he'd give it to her. He turned his face into the pillow to smile.

"Tell me," she said. "Tell me."

"I shot a man in Montana once. I hit him in the belly."

"Yes," she said. He felt her nails dig into his skin.

"He'd fired twice at me, but it was across a street, and he was shooting for my head. He missed." One of her hands moved down across his naked hip, hot against his skin. "I shot at him and missed him. Then I shot at him again and hit him in the belly. He was turned to the side a little and the bullet tore him open." Her warm hand gripped at his hip. Lea felt the nails scratching. "He turned and tried to walk away. A lot of men do that when they're hurt bad. As if they can walk away from the pain, I guess."

Her hand was still. Lea felt something warm touching the swollen red scar. He stiffened, his cock rising hard against the sheet. He heard a soft sound, felt the quick motion along the wound.

She was licking it.

"Then . . . then his guts came out. You could see

116

them coming out with all the blood. A coil of it came out of him, sticky and blue-white in the blood. It was hanging down onto his pants.''

Her hand slid down his belly and found his cock. She was squeezing, her hand moving slowly up and down under the sheet.

"I would have shot him again, but a woman was in the way. She came running out in the street and got in the way."

Lea heard the German woman moan. He felt her trembling as she bent over him. Her tongue was frantic as she licked at the scar; he felt her teeth against the stitches.

Then he turned.

"No," she said, and her hand left his swollen cock. Her face was flush, and a strand of hair had come loose and trailed across her forehead. Her mouth was wet.

She tried to stand, but he reached up and took her by the arms and held her. She tried to pull away, but he wouldn't let her go.

"I haven't finished," he said. "There's more to tell you, about how that man died."

She moaned something in German and turned her head away.

"No, no," Lea said. "I haven't finished—and you haven't, either."

He pulled her back down to the side of the bed, gripping her arms hard enough to hurt her. Then he reached up with one hand to touch the hair gathered at the back of her neck. He held her there. Then, with his other hand, he took her slender wrist—as slim as a child's—and forced her hand under the sheet to his cock. She kept her fist clenched against him there for a

117

moment, then her hand slowly opened and her fingers curled around him.

"If I do this, will you let me go?"

The small hand gripped gently, squeezed, stroked. He looked up and saw her staring at him, her pale eyes wide.

"I haven't finished what I was telling you," Lea said.

"I don't want to hear."

"Yes, you do," Lea said. "You want to hear it all." Her smiled at her. "You want to see something, too, don't you?"

He let go of her wrist, picked up the top of the sheet, and threw it back.

She stared at him for a moment more, looking into his eyes. Then she looked down at his cock, standing red and swollen, laced with knotted veins, thrusting up out of the narrow grip of her white fingers.

"That's what you like, isn't it?"

She didn't say anything. She just sat beside him, staring down at him, at her hand.

"You like licking things," Lea said. "Then go ahead and lick that."

She shook her head without saying a word. He saw that she was starting to cry. He tightened his grip on her hair, gathering it in his fingers at the back of her neck; then, slowly, he forced her head down. She tried to twist away, to get off the edge of the bed and stand up, but Lea tightened his grip until she cried out with the pain.

The bulging red head of it touched her cheek, left a pale smear across it. Lea had both hands on her head now, guiding her. He brought her back, brought her lips down to it. She sobbed, opened her mouth, and took it.

Lea felt her teeth against it, the heat and slippery wetness of her mouth.

She still held the shaft in her hand, and now, angry and frightened, she squeezed harder. Lea felt some juice rise in it.

He held her still there, hunched over him, the nape of her neck shining like white silk in the lamplight. There was a faint dusting of hair down along the back of her slender neck.

She was trembling, breathing heavily through her nose. Lea could see the bulge of his cock in her mouth. Her pale cheek ballooned, her mouth stretched achingly wide. He felt her tongue move against him.

"Be still," Lea said to her. "And listen to me."

She groaned, struggled a moment more, and then was quiet.

"When the woman came out and got in the way," Lea said, "I walked on across the street to them. He'd already gone down. I could see him sitting in the dirt beside the boardwalk. You ever seen a pig butchered? He was sitting down in a big puddle of blood, and his guts were out into his lap. He had his arms around them, the way you'd hold a baby in your lap. I guess to keep them out of the dirt."

The German woman moaned and moved under his hands. Then he felt her tongue begin to move against the head of his cock.

"The woman came at me, to try and keep me away from him, I had to shove her aside. I walked up to him. He was already half gone; just stepping up close to him, I was walking in the blood."

Her head began to move slowly, up and down. Gulping, swallowing, she began to suck on him, her

119

hand shaking as she held him. His cock was wet now, soaked with her saliva. She was slobbering over it, gasping for breath.

"He'd been a handsome man, this one. Tried to look like Hickock, I guess. A fancy dresser—a sport with two guns, long hair, and a silk vest."

Lea bit his lip and heaved up against her. He felt it coming. They were sweating now. Her face was flush with blood, with effort, as she pulled and sucked at him as if she were starving for it.

"Oh, you bitch! Take it! Here it comes for you!" He groaned with the pleasure of it. It was coming out of him as she sucked, moaning and shaking her head as she worked on him.

"Take it the way *he* took it. He looked up at me as if I was going to help him. As if I was going to put his guts back for him. Ah, Christ!" Lea tried to hold her, to keep her from sucking so hard, so fast. It was hurting him it felt so good.

"He looked up at me with his damned long hair in his eyes, looking for some kind of help. I put the barrel against that bastard's head . . . and I cocked the piece . . . and . . . I . . . blew . . . his . . . God-damned *brains* out!"

Lea groaned through clenched teeth, heaved, and thrust up into her. And he came.

Moaning, he let it go. He let everything go. Let it flow into her mouth.

She took it—drinking, sucking, and swallowing again —and bent further to lick, and lap it up where it had run.

120

CHAPTER FOURTEEN

She cleaned him the way a cat cleans her kittens. He'd let go of her and lay back onto the pillows, watching her. She was very thorough.

When she was finished, he reached down and pulled her up to him, kissing her throat, and mouth, and eyes.

"You darling," he said. "You're a beauty, aren't you?"

She smiled against his chest. "A whore is what my brother would say." She turned her head to look at him. "And you were very cruel to me."

"And it's usually the other way 'round?"

"Usually," she said, and bared her teeth to nip at a fold of his skin, biting down hard.

"Ouch!"

"See." Her teethmarks were red on his skin. "I have my revenge."

Lea reached down to pull up her full skirt, sliding his hand up the slim, silk-stockinged legs.

"But not your pleasure, I think."

"Oh, yes," she said.

121

And a moment later, sliding his hand high up between smooth, cool, slender thighs, he felt a hot, tangled little patch of fur.

"Yes," he said.

"But play with me a little, my killer of men."

Sarah Bridge came in and woke him at noon. Dr. Edwards and Leo Drexel were with her.

Lea felt fine, almost well enough to get out of bed.

"Any reason I shouldn't get up, doctor?"

"No, you can get up now if you like, though another day in bed wouldn't hurt you." Edwards checked both wounds—the small cut on Lea's chest, the longer, stitched scar down his left side. "Damned lucky, Mr. Lea, I'll say that. Although from the looks of the scars already on you, this sort of injury appears to be fairly common for you."

Lea grunted and let him get on with his work. He was watching Sarah Bridge at the window, putting a fresh bouquet of flowers into the vase on a small table there. He had a momentary vision of her lying across the bed, as the Baron's sister had lain there just a few hours before, her skirts thrown up, her knees high, legs spread wide, gasping with pleasure while he did to her what he'd done to Erica.

She turned back from the window, smiling at him, and Lea felt suddenly embarrassed at what he'd been thinking. What the hell. She was Abe's daughter, and she'd been damn good to him while he was lying around half out of his head. There was more to this girl than her cunt.

"Good God!" Drexel was watching over the doctor's shoulder as he dressed the wound on Lea's side. "That

122

looks dreadful!" Drexel turned pale and looked away.

"Leo," Edwards said, "if you're going to be sick, leave the room."

"I am not going to be sick, doctor," Drexel said with a sniff, and he walked over to the fireplace and sat down in one of the armchairs.

Edwards finished his bandaging, then fished a small bottle of tonic out of his leather bag and handed it to Lea. "Take a spoonful three times a day until it's gone." He closed up his bag, nodded to Sarah, and walked out.

"By God, he's in a hurry," Drexel said.

Sarah laughed. "Two Austrians asked him to go climbing with them this side of High Pass this afternoon. I think he was afraid he was going to miss them."

"What Austrians?" Drexel said.

"Those brothers—the Erlingens."

"Oh, those two. I'm not surprised. *Mountain climbers.*" He shrugged.

"Mr. Lea," Sarah said. "My father . . . well, if you're feeling up to it, he'd like to see you."

"Fine," Lea said, and sat up. Then he remembered his naked chest, and lay back down. "Let him come."

Drexel laughed. "Behold, modesty."

"Oh, Leo! Well, Mr. Lea, you see, he thought you might still be angry with him for what happened."

"No," Lea said, "I'm not angry with him. It looked bad enough for any man to think I'd killed her."

She smiled at him. "Well, I'll go and tell him to come up." When she was at the door, Lea called after her.

"Miss Bridge."

"Yes?"

"I just . . . I just wanted to thank you . . . for taking care of me. It was very nice of you."

"Oh, we take care of all our people at Gunstock, Mr. Lea." She smiled again, and was gone.

"I think you're outclassed, Lea," Drexel said from the armchair.

"I don't doubt it." Lea threw back the sheet, swung his feet out of the bed, and sat on the edge for a moment. He thought he'd feel a little dizzy, after being flat on his back for almost a week, but he didn't. He felt fine.

When he stood up Drexel had to catch him as he staggered and fell against the bedside table. The water glass rolled off the table's edge and onto the carpet. Drexel had moved pretty fast to get there so quickly.

"That was stupid," Drexel said. "You should have let me help you."

The giddiness had passed, but Lea had to sit back down on the bed. His side hurt like hell. All that exercise with the Baron's sister hadn't bothered it at all, but standing had seemed to tear the wound apart all over again. He glanced down at his side, at the bandage.

"No," Drexel said, "it isn't bleeding." He sighed. "Listen. If you don't mind, why don't I help you get your clothes on. Otherwise it'll take you all afternoon."

Lea knew what that "if you don't mind" was about. He was stark naked, and Leo Drexel was a sissy. But there were worse things to be than a sissy.

"I think," he said, "I saw my clothes hanging in that closet over there. But God knows what they did with my underwear."

When Lea was finally dressed and sitting down in an armchair beside the fireplace, he was damned glad to be there. They'd brought his Sunday best black suit, shirt, and other clothes over from the cabin.

The side didn't hurt so badly, now, although it was still stiff and sore. But the weakness bothered him. A few years ago, a couple of cuts—even as bad as these—and he'd have been in bed maybe a day and a night, and that would have been it. He would have been up and riding by now.

Drexel sat for a moment, staring at Lea. Then he smiled.

"Uh, tell me, Mr. Lea, have you spent quite *all* your time shooting wild animals, and, I suppose, people?"

"Not quite all my time."

"Ah, yes . . . I see. You've been something of a sport, then? San Francisco, I suppose?"

"And Chicago."

Drexel nodded. "Good! I'm very happy to hear it." He looked into the fire for a few moments. "Because I believe that Gunstock—and the estimable Bridges—may be falling into some very deep difficulties indeed. Difficulties requiring quick wits, as well as a strong right arm."

Lea said nothing. He'd always found it best to let the other man talk himself out—if he was talking about trouble. He had nothing against Drexel; from what he'd heard in the kitchens and stables, the elegant sissy was a decent enough fellow, and a friend of the Bridges. Maybe he was.

"You have nothing to say?" Drexel said. "That's surprising. You surely don't believe, for example, that that very unpleasant Mr. Budreau, who—*ventilated* I think is the term—who ventilated you with his trusty Barlow knife, did so out of a murderous jealousy?" He smiled at Lea, and carefully smoothed the wrinkled sleeve of his suit coat. "Say what you will of the noble red man," he said, gazing at the rumpled cloth, frowning, "he makes a disasterous valet."

"And why," said Lea, "wouldn't Budreau have been jealous enough to have killed Edna and then come for me? He might have been with her. A couple of others were."

"Tsk, tsk. Unchivalrous, Mr. Lea. And wide of the mark." Satisfied with the sleeve at last, he looked up at Lea. "The ferocious Mr. Budreau didn't care a hoot about that young lady—or about *any* young lady." He shrugged. "Budreau was of *my* persuasion." He smiled. "Not, I hasten to add, that I know that from personal experience. Let us say, rather, that I have a nose for it." His faded blue eyes sharpened, watching Lea's face. "Did you know that? Did you know it all along?"

"No," Lea said. "Not that. But I knew it wasn't a personal matter."

"Pretty god-damned personal, I'd say! To try and cut a man's guts out! And choke a pretty girl to death!" Abe Bridge was a quiet walker, and the thick Gunstock carpets had ushered him into the room silently. Lea didn't like that kind of surprise. He'd remember from now on how softly a man could walk on fine Oriental rugs.

But Abe had heard what he'd said and Drexel was already guessing. The cat was halfway out of the bag; might as well show it clear, nose to tail.

"No, Mr. Bridge," he said. "Not personal at all." Out of the corner of his eye, he saw Drexel nod. Abe stood in the shadows of the open doorway, feet planted wide apart, as if he'd grown from the Gunstock floorboards, and glowered down at Lea with an odd look on his face.

"Budreau was *hired* to try for me—probably hired to kill Edna first, then clean me up too, in case she'd talked too much in bed." Lea paused for a moment, then said softly, "She had, poor baby. I should have known she wouldn't leave it alone."

Abe reached behind him to swing the door shut.

"Leave what alone?" he said.

"What indeed?" said Leo Drexel.

"Edna was cleaning a room in Mr. Larrabee's suite," Lea said. "She told me she overheard Larrabee and Count Orloff in a conversation about a silver deposit in the mountains."

"Where?" said Abe. "What silver?"

"At the railway cut, down by Little River."

"She was lying—poor girl—there is no damn silver in these mountains. And, by God, I ought to know!"

"Larrabee's surveyors told him they found some—a heavy lode of it, too—when they dynamited down there. I'd say they know their business." Lea said. "At least Larrabee believed it. He only has railroad rights there. It's your mountain."

"Damn right," Abe growled. "And he paid through the nose for those rail rights, I can tell you."

"Well, it seems, Abe," Drexel drawled, "that he's decided to improve his investment." He glanced at Lea. "By doing precisely what, Mr. Lea?"

"Edna said he'd hired the Count and his Cossacks to ruin Gunstock—probably so that you'd have no choice but to sell the whole shebang to him dirt cheap. That would leave Mr. Larrabee controlling a mountain full of silver."

Abe snorted. "Some yarn! I don't believe a word of it! These Irish girls are full of dreams and blarney. The

127

poor girl dreamed it. That's all there is to it!''

"And they had her murdered for her Irish imagination, I suppose," Drexel said. "It won't do, Abe."

Abe turned on him. "Well? And what do you suppose Count Yuri Orloff is doing in this plot, then? The man's a *Count,* for God's sake! He owns more land than you can ride across in a week!"

"Abe, a man can own all the land in the world and still be desperate for cold, hard cash." Drexel turned to Lea. "Did the girl say how much the old man offered our fine Russian Count?"

"A million in gold," Lea said.

There was a little pause, then Abe reached out to the rocking chair, dragged it over nearer to the fire, and sat with a grunt. He looked suddenly older in the shifting light of the burning hickory logs.

"My God," he said. "Why the hell is it so dark in here? It's only afternoon! Draw those damn curtains, will you, Leo? Let's have some sunlight!" He turned to Lea. "So why did they kill her? Answer me that!"

"She went back to try and get money from them, I think," Lea said.

"Poor girl," Drexel said, pulling the velvet curtains wide. "Poor little girl."

Sunlight flooded the room.

CHAPTER FIFTEEN

Lea moved back into his cabin that night, and found Tocsen waiting there. The old Shoshone just nodded with a grunt when Lea walked in, sitting cross-legged on his smelly bedroll in front of the pot-belly stove. The old Indian had stoked the stove red-hot against the deep chill of the mountain autumn, and, having grunted his greeting to Lea, he returned to rocking slightly back and forth, muttering to himself and puffing on a cracked briar pipe he had picked out of the Gunstock dump. The big double-barreled Greener twelve-gauge was lying on the bedroll beside him. Lea had a notion the old man was playing bodyguard.

He was not unwelcome either. Lea was worn out. Just sitting on his butt talking to Abe and Drexel for a few hours while they tried to figure a checkmate to Larrabee's plan had worn him to a frazzle. The beefsteak dinner sent up from the kitchens had helped —but not enough. Lea needed a solid night's sleep; he needed it badly. A long, sweet sleep, with someone to keep watch for him while he had it. Lea didn't think for a minute that Larrabee had forgotten about him—and knew damn well that that fat old son-of-a-bitch had been told of the meeting Lea'd had with Abe and Drexel. Larrabee was the kind who made sure he was informed.

No, Larrabee wouldn't forget about Lea. That was just as well for him, because Lea had no intention of forgetting—or forgiving—old man Larrabee. The old millionaire must have thought that having a little Irish maidservant killed was nothing but a minor business inconvenience. It was a misjudgement that Larrabee wouldn't live long enough to regret.

Lea sat on the narrow cot, biting his lip against the sharp pain stabbing up along his side as he wrestled his suit-coat and shirt off. Sitting there, he noticed that someone had freshly sanded and scrubbed the cabin floor. Done a good job too. The stains were hardly noticeable. There was a soft knock on the door.

Old Tocsen was a rare one, no doubt about it. The moment the knock sounded, the old man had casually picked up the Greener, cocked the hammers and, still squatting on his bedroll, swung both barrels around to cover the cabin's only window. A rare old man, Lea thought, and smiled.

He slid his Bisley Colt out from under the cot's hard pillow and called out: "Come on in."

Sarah Bridge swung the door open and walked in, her skirts rustling, bringing a breath of cold night air in with her.

When she'd closed the door behind her, and lowered the latch, Lea slid the Colt back under the pillow. A moment later, Tocsen lowered the Greener, muttering, and eased the twin hammers.

130

"Mr. Lea."

Lea got up off the cot and gestured toward it. "Here, sit down."

"No thank you." She stood beside old Tocsen at the stove, warming her slender hands over the dull cherry glow. "I . . . Mr. Lea—"

"Just Lea'll do."

"Very well . . . *Lea.*"

"Your father's talked to you?"

She turned from the stove to face him, her face drawn with worry. "Yes, he has. He and Leo, both. I . . . I didn't want to believe . . ."

"That sweet old Mr. Larrabee would do such a thing?"

She flushed. "Well, I didn't *want* to think it, I suppose . . ." She glanced at him. "We . . . we could all be mistaken about this, after all."

"Could be."

"Well, we *could!* Mr. Larrabee is an old man, and a very important man too. He's *very* rich and important. He's a friend of the President! So I don't see why in the world—"

"And how do you think Larrabee got to *be* so all-fired important, Miss Bridge? Knitting mittens for the poor?"

She drew herself up. "I'm not trying to be amusing, *Mr.* Lea."

"No," Lea said, and he sat back down on the cot to pull off his boots. "There's not a damn—pardon me—thing funny about it. Ask Edna O'Malley. Ask Budreau for that matter."

She looked down at her clasped hands. "I . . . I know. I know you were fond of Edna." She looked up. "But . . . but you see, my father is riding out tomorrow.

131

He's taking six of the hands with him and riding down to Little River to see for himself about that silver that you—''

''That I say is there?'' Lea pulled off one of his boots with a pained grunt.

''Yes.''

Lea wrestled with his second boot. The son-of-a-bitch didn't want to come off! And his side felt as if it were on fire. With a sweep of her skirts, Sarah came to the cot, knelt, and gripping the boot, tugged it off his foot.

''Thanks.''

''Mr. Lea—''

''Lea.''

''*Lea.* You shouldn't even have been out of bed today.''

''Let alone feeding your father that cock-an'-bull yarn?''

She stood looking down at him, her dark blue eyes steady on his. ''I'm worried about him, Mis—Lea. I'm worried that he will be made to look a fool if there's no silver down at Little River.''

''And you're worried he'll be killed out there if there is.''

''Yes.''

''Well, Abe *could* get killed out there, Miss Bridge. I offered to go with him.''

Sarah began to pace in the cabin's cramped space. Old Tocsen turned his head to watch her, puffing his pipe, his heavy-lidded old eyes following her. White women were restless; that was certainly true.

''Oh, you couldn't go with him. He was right not to let you. You won't be able to ride for days.''

132

"He has six men with him?"

"Yes."

"And the Count and those Cossacks of his are staying put?"

"Leo said there was no sign of their leaving."

"Fine. As long as Orloff's not out there, Abe will be all right."

She stopped pacing. "Yes, I suppose you're right. He has taken good men with him: Folliard, Tiny Morgan, and a man named Johnson who they say is good with a gun."

"Nothing out there to bother them," Lea said, "as long as Orloff stays at Gunstock."

"Yes. Leo's having people watch him and those men of his." She stopped pacing, glanced at him, and frowned. "Oh, Lea, I'd forgotten how ill you'd been. I'm terribly sorry! You need rest, not to be bothered with *my* worries." She went to the door. "I'll leave you, and let you sleep. Do you need anything? Do you have Dr. Edward's medicine?"

"I've got it."

"Well, then . . ." She unlatched the door, and turned, smiling. "I apologize for troubling you with all this. Good night. Good night, Tocsen."

The old Indian grunted in reply, and Sarah swung the cabin door open, went out, and shut it behind her.

A nice girl, Lea thought. And damn right to be worried about old Abe. Probably a mistake for the old man to leave Gunstock right now. Might have been better to have waited Larrabee out, handled the Russians here, on his own ground.

Lea sighed and stood up with a grunt to unbutton his trousers. Not a damn thing *he* could do about it anyway.

Abe would do what Abe would do.

"Restless Flower Eye." Tocsen said, staring into the fire in the potbelly stove.

"What?"

But the old man had nothing more to say.

Lea dreamed of Edna. "My God," he said to her in the dream, "I leave everyone dead behind me, as if I were death himself." She looked at him as if he'd gone crazy, and laughed. She was sitting up in a bed somewhere. Her breasts were bare.

"Do you know he looked at me?" she said.

"Who?" Lea said in the dream. "Who looked at you?"

"That little Rooshin," Edna said to him. "He stood underneath a tree and watched while Budreau choked the life right out of me."

"Oh, don't worry about him," Lea said to her, and she smiled and reached down to stroke her nipples. "I'll kill him. I'll kill them all. Didn't I kill Budreau? Didn't I put a knife into his throat?"

"You choked the German woman," Edna said, and pouted. "I know that well enough!"

"I couldn't help it," Lea said to her.

"He can't help anything," the smiling man said, and he walked through the room and out the door.

"Tell me what it's like to be dead, Edna," Lea said. "Do you still know you are Edna?"

"I know nothin'," Edna said to him. . . .

Lea woke early in the morning. Old Tocsen was snoring beside the potbelly stove. Lea felt better than he had since the fight with Budreau. The stitches itched along his side, but the muscles there didn't hurt. He felt a little stiff, but all right.

He got up and dressed in his boots, jean trousers, a wool shirt and his buckskin vest. When he sat on the bed and stomped his boots on, Tocsen woke up and stared at him, blinking.

"Come on and let's get something to eat," Lea said. He strapped on the Bisley Colt and found his Arkansas toothpick lying on the little cane-bottom chair beside the bed.

"I keep for you. It sharp." The old Indian rolled back over on his side and began to go back to sleep.

"Thanks." Lea slid the knife down into his right boot.

He unlatched the door and stepped outside. It was a cold, clear morning. Smoke trailed across the blue sky from the towering chimneys of the hotel looming across the stable yards.

Lea walked across the cobbles to the kitchen garden, and on up the path. He was walking with his head down, thinking, and he heard boots coming down the path toward him. He looked up and saw one of Orloff's Cossacks coming down the path toward him from the kitchen. The Cossack was chewing on a chunk of bread.

Lea recognized the man, but didn't remember his name. He was a tall, bony-looking man with lank dirty-blond hair, and a full beard, like the rest of them.

The Cossack glanced down the path at Lea as he came. He had greenish eyes and his face was gray with dirt.

From that look, and the way he was walking, Lea saw that the man intended to walk him off the narrow path. The Cossack didn't have a saber, but he was carrying a big pistol in a closed holster on his belt. A Nagent, it looked like; maybe some big European pistol.

He swallowed the last of the bread and walked fast, straight toward Lea, swinging his arms. He stared into Lea's eyes, grinning at him.

Just before the Cossack reached him, just as Lea sensed the man bracing himself, lowering his shoulder for the impact, Lea side-stepped to the right, well off the path, smiled, and tipped his Stetson as the Cossack went striding past.

The Cossack turned his head to stare at Lea, and laughed. Then he walked on his way and didn't look back.

Lea went up the path to the kitchen and down past the row of salad tables, where people were already laying out the garden stuff to be cleaned and cut and arranged for lunch. He was turning into the doorway to the servants' dining room when he heard chef de la Maine calling his name.

Lea stood and waited while the big Frenchman bellied past a dozen scullions running back and forth with pots and pans—Indian girls, most of them—and came up to Lea with his flour-white hand out and a big smile on his face.

"So good!" he said, and took Lea's hand and pumped it hard. "So good!" He nodded at Lea, and winked. *"Tres bien!"* He made a slicing gesture with his free hand. "You 'av cut that Budreau well, no? For his killing la petite Edna!" He nodded again, and his tall chef's hat bobbed on his head. "You go in to the dining room, an' I will per-r-rsonally bring br-r-reakfast."

Lea smiled and nodded, took his hand back—the chef was a strong man—and went into the dining room and

136

sat down. Three chambermaids were sitting across the table. He knew one of them, a girl named Patty Burke, but they didn't say anything to him, just stared and whispered back and forth.

After a considerable while, and Lea getting hungrier by the minute, Old Tocsen looked around the corner of the dining-room door, then shuffled in to sit beside Lea at the table. The maids had already left. Tocsen sighed and farted, then sat waiting for breakfast, muttering to himself.

De la Maine came in with a tray, smiling. The smile turned a little sour when he saw Tocsen sitting at the table. He rolled his eyes. *"Alors, la belle sauvage!"* He set the tray down before them. There was a plate of lamb-chops, each with a little white cuff of paper, curled strips of bacon, a big omelet that smelled of cheese and green herbs, and a hot cake with white icing and raisins. It all smelled wonderful.

Lea got up and shook de la Maine's hand again. It was not a small thing for the chef to cook something special for one person. Lea had eaten fine French cooking before. But not often.

Between the two of them, he and Tocsen cleared the tray. Lea ate the bacon, and the omelet, and the cake. The Shoshone ate all the lamb-chops.

CHAPTER SIXTEEN

When he finished breakfast, Lea left the old Shoshone sitting there chewing on the lamb-chop bones, and walked out through the passage under the main staircase to go to the gun-room. Tocsen had told him that Davies had taken some guests out bird-shooting while he was sick from the fight with Budreau. Lea didn't think he'd be taking many more guests out hunting from Gunstock. And Davies, who was head wrangler and a good hunter to boot, had probably handled everything all right. But it wouldn't hurt to check.

He dug in his buckskin jacket pocket for the key, and unlocked the heavy oak door.

It was a big narrow room, with a long mahogany table, covered with an oil-stained canvas tarp, running down the center, between two glass-cased walls of guns. Almost three hundred guns altogether. The room smelled of gun oil, and the cleaning table was littered with patches, rods, oil cans and bore brushes. Davies was a good hunter, but he still had something to learn about keeping a gun room. At this rate, it would be a pigpen in a week. He'd have to talk to Davies.

Lea got to work cleaning up. It was work he'd done a hundred times; work he didn't even have to think about. It left him free to think about other things. Like packing up, getting the old dun out of the stable, and making tracks the hell out of Gunstock. He'd been out and gone once—and had come back when the old man called. He'd owed Abe that much, for giving him the job. Well, he'd come back, and now he'd killed the bully who'd killed Edna.

What now? A stand-up fight against those Cossacks? Against Larrabee and his millions? No way for him to win there—even if he got lucky. Win? Kill a Russian Count . . . kill Larrabee . . . Do that, and every newspaper reporter, every peace officer in three states would be out to get him. Hell, the U.S. Army'd be sent out!

The name of *Farris Lea* wouldn't stand long under that light. It would be Buckskin Frank Leslie before you could shake a stick! They'd hunt him, they'd catch him, and they'd hang him high as Haman.

Moving on was the thing to do.

Lea leaned over the gleaming mahogany, rubbing the soft wax into the dark, shining wood with hard, forceful sweeps of his arm. The table top was dark and as reflective as dark water in the soft glow of gas lights.

So why the hell wasn't he gone already? Edwards had said the stitches needed to come out of his chest and side in about ten days, but any frontier saw-bones could pick those out of him. He could do that himself, in fact he *had* done it.

Lea put the can of wax away, pulled a clean square of chamois from the drawer, and began to polish the table, avoiding the eyes of his reflection as he slowly worked his way down the glossy length of wood. As he worked, he felt the faint tug and ache of the healing wound along his side. Cut to the muscle, Edwards had said. The chest wound wasn't so bad. Budreau had tried for the heart there, and got a rib instead.

The table was finished. A damn good job. And Davies could damn well do it from now on . . .

Lea knew he wasn't going to leave Gunstock. Not yet.

He was staying because he wanted to stay. Not to help Abe, though that was part of it. And not to help Abe's daughter, though that was part of it too.

The real reason was what it had always been. He wanted them to know. He wanted all of them: Abe, Sarah, that Russian Count, and old man Larrabee, to know exactly who he was!

He wanted them to know the way Budreau had known, standing with that knife in his throat.

He didn't want to run anymore. He was finished with running. He had left so much behind him. There was almost nothing left of Frank Leslie.

There was a soft knock on the gun-room door. Lea stood clear of the long table. "Yes?"

"Lea?" It was Leo Drexel.

Lea slid back the bolt and slowly swung the heavy door open. Drexel stood in the doorway, slender, elegant in a fine gray suit. One eyebrow was raised.

"Being careful who knocks?" He smiled. "Very sensible, Lea." He strolled into the room and leaned against one of the gun cabinets while Lea closed the door and bolted it. "I have news. Nothing spectacular, I suppose, but interesting."

"What is it?"

"Well, you understand, in Gunstock I have my sources." He turned to examine his reflection in the gun-case glass, adjusted his cravat.

"Yes?"

"It seems that our notable Mr. Larrabee has taken *steps*. He has, in fact, sent his valet to the gardener's shed to hire a boy to ride to Salmon Station with a telegram." He stepped back so that he could view his whole reflection in the glass front of the case. "Not bad," he said, and nodded at it.

Lea didn't say anything. He stood, waiting for Drexel to tell him.

Drexel turned from the glass. He wasn't smiling anymore. "That telegram said, and I quote, 'To Henry Buskirk, Santa Fe. Send Shannon Gunstock soonest. Repeat, soonest.' "

Drexel stood staring at Lea. "Now," he said, "why that little message should strike me as ominous, I don't know, except perhaps that it is so simple. A man like Larrabee could send for an army, if he chose."

"He's a quieter man than that, I think," Lea said.

"Yes. Then who, or what, is "Shannon?"

Lea stood, thinking, looking past Drexel to the tall, heavily curtained window at the end of the room.

Lea had known a man named Shannon once. A big, thick-bellied, bearded man. Partner in a freight outfit in Colorado. Surely nothing to do with this.

The only other Shannon he'd heard of was a gunman. If it was the same fellow, he'd been in a shooting in Wyoming years ago. Killed Slim Wilson out of Cheyenne.

Lea had met Wilson once, a long time ago. If this

141

Shannon was a shooter, and the same man, then h[e]
must be very good, if the years hadn't slowed hi[m]
down. That shooting in Wyoming had been a long tim[e]
ago—more than ten years ago.

"What do you think, Mr. Lea?" said Drexel. H[e]
wasn't playing the fine sissy now. He looked like [a]
worried man.

"Well, I think he's probably sent for a violent ma[n.]
Probably would have, in any case, to balance off thos[e]
Cossacks of Orloff's. Men like Larrabee like to have a[n]
ace in the hole."

"And this Shannon?"

"Must be an ace," Lea said, and smiled. "Wouldn't b[e]
sent for otherwise."

"Yes." Drexel frowned. "So I thought, too."

"How soon—"

"The fastest," Drexel said, speaking with the confi[-]
dence of a man who's made countless travel arrange[-]
ments for countless spoiled, impatient, and influencia[l]
guests, "and damn the Southern Pacific Railroad an[d]
the Idaho spur—the fastest he can travel, for Larrabe[e]
or God almighty, will get him to Gunstock in six days a[t]
the earliest."

"Only six days from New Mexico!"

Drexel smiled sadly. "That's why I damned the Idah[o]
spur. That line was built out to Salmon Station year[s]
ago."

"But just for beef and freight—and barely once [a]
week at that!"

"Unless someone with a great deal of influence, M[r.]
Lea, were to ask them to route up a special . . ." Drexe[l]
sighed. And Lea knew he was dead right. He'd be a[t]
Gunstock in six days.

142

When they left the gun-room, Drexel had shaken hands with him, a little mournfully, Lea thought, and left him to go out into the grand pavilion alongside the lobby. Lea turned back down the passageway under the wide staircase, stepped out into the corridor leading back to the servants' hall—and ran straight into a damn gaggle of guests.

Young girls, most of them—a girl named Maxine Budweiser, who's father was supposed to be a big brewer in the east, and four other girls Lea didn't know —all of them goggling at him, their eyes as big as saucers. The dangerous man, the *killer*, had suddenly appeared before them.

They were pretty girls—Maxine was anyway—and not one of them a day over seventeen. All of them ruffled up in muslin and taffeta or whatever. But to Lea they seemed like a herd of silly heifers, the way they stood huddled together goggling at him.

Toby Easterby—for once giving up on the older, faster ladies—was squiring the bunch of them around. Another boy, Arthur, was hovering around too.

"Good day, ladies," Lea said, and gave them his best smile and bow. Watch the sparrows scatter.

And scatter they did—in a flustered flurry of sqeaks and chirps and hasty curtsies, midway between manners and terror.

Easterby and Arthur finally herded them together and away, Easterby grinning over his shoulder to Lea as they went.

When Abe got back—*if* Abe got back—he'd probably get an earful from a few mamas about allowing bravos and butchers to patrol the halls of Gunstock, to frighten their little girls.

143

As he started down the flight of steps to the servants' hall, Lea thought of Edna for a moment.

Edna had been seventeen years old. It was a young age to die.

"Me darlin' " she'd said to him once, lying naked as a baby on him, and covered with sweat from their fucking, "Me darlin', you're damn near as good as auld Fadder McFee."

How they'd laughed.

" . . . damned near as good as Fadder McFee!" Lea started laughing now, and met Sarah Bridge coming up the stairs.

She frowned up at him, and he went down two steps more, to her level. Her blue eyes were sparkling with anger.

"If Mr. Drexel has spoken to you, Mr. Lea, I'm at a loss to know what you find funny about the matter!"

Well, Drexel wasn't keeping secrets from the lady of the house. And the lady looked mighty worried about it, as well she might.

"I wasn't laughing about the arrival of Mr. Larrabee's hoodlum, Miss Bridge." He saw the worry carved into tiny lines at the corner of her mouth and eyes. "Or about the spot your father may get into, either."

"I . . . I know."

"Orloff and his men are still here, aren't they?"

"Yes . . . yes, they are."

Her head was down, her face shadowed under the dim staircase light. Lea saw she was starting to weep.

He hesitated a moment, then put his hand on her arm.

"Listen Sarah, Abe isn't going to get hurt as long as

those Russians stay put. He must be nearly to Little River by now. It won't take him long to find the silver ore, if it's there. Then he'll be on his way back. You'll see him again in two or three days."

"Oh, I know he'll be all right." She took out her handkerchief, dabbed at her eyes, then blew her nose. "I know you think I'm being a silly fool." She shook her head and looked up at him, trying to smile. "Abe . . . Abe would be furious if he knew I was so frightened for him! Daddy thinks he can handle anything!"

"I think he can too," Lea said, and smiled at her.

"Yes." She sniffed and put her handkerchief away. "But Mr. Larrabee and that dreadful little Russian. They . . . they're different!"

"A loftier sort of skunk, you mean?"

She giggled. "Yes, I suppose I do mean that."

"I don't mean to make light of them," Lea said, "or to make light of the trouble your father might be in. But I'll tell you this: there is no way that Larrabee, or the Russian is going to be taking Gunstock away from you."

She looked up into his face. "Thank you, Mr. Lea. I know that you mean it. I thank you for staying to help us." She smiled, wryly. "Particularly after I made such a cake of myself, ordering you off the place when the Baron got shot!"

Lea laughed. "Well, you weren't far wrong at that. I was the guide. I was responsible for getting him shot!"

"No." She blushed. "It wasn't your fault at all. I lost my temper, that's all."

"Well, if you'll forgive me, I'll forgive you."

"All right." She glanced up at him. "I forgive you."

What a good-looking girl you are, Lea thought. Their eyes met.

"Thank you, Miss Bridge," he said. And he bent down and kissed her gently on the mouth.

CHAPTER SEVENTEEN

Her lips were cool and slightly parted. He thought, just for a moment, that she pressed her mouth against him. He felt heat, wetness. Then it was gone. She turned, brushed past him with a rustle of skirts, and went up the stairs.

That afternoon, Lea went out to the cabin and gathered up an armful of dirty clothes, his extra pair of boots, and his soap and razor. Then he went over to the Chinaman's.

It was generally supposed at Gunstock that all four of the fat, sturdy Chinese women working for old Chun in the laundry shed were his wives. Chinese were known for multiplication in that field, and each of the four certainly treated the old man with the bullying lack of respect proper to a wife. Chinese women were just as hard on the Indian girls who helped them stir the huge laundry tubs and work the big newfangled steam-mangles that Abe had had freighted in all the way from Boise.

Lea walked down the long stone flagway. The laundry shed was behind a planted row of loblolly pines, out past the kitchen gardens. He climbed the steps to the big corrugated iron door, and swung it open.

Walking into the laundry shed was a little like walking into hell—blazing hot, swirling with clouds of steam, and noisy with the hiss and whistle of the big boiler powering the mangles, and the screams and curses of Chun's four wives.

"What you need, Mr. Lea?" Chun had come out of the wall of gray like a Chinese ghost.

"Laundry . . . bath . . . shave."

Chun made an exasperated face. "Busy . . . busy . . . busy!"

"Then I'll come back tonight."

"No, no!" The old Chinaman's goatee was dripping sweat and condensed steam. "You give!" He snatched Lea's laundry bundle out from under his arm, and ducked away, back into the steam. "You come on!"

Lea followed him into the fog.

Chun led him through the steam-filled laundry, through a door, and into another room lined with long tables where Indian girls were ironing and folding from heaping baskets of fresh wash.

Then they went through another door into a small room behind the boiler. Big cast-iron washtubs stood in ranks against the wall. The little room was soaking with water condensed from the steamy air.

"Bath!" said Chun, and he pointed to the first tub in the row. Lea looked into the tub, and was relieved to see it was empty. The last bath he'd had at Chun's he'd shared with several dirty sheets. Chun walked out, taking Lea's laundry with him. Lea undressed, pulling his boots off with a grunt. He still felt the side when he did that. He stuck the toothpick point first into the dark, soaked wood beside the tub, and hung the Bisley Colt from a peg over it. They'd both need cleaning and oiling after sitting around in this steambath, but they had to be handy: a bathhouse was a very good place to surprise and kill a man.

Naked, Lea stepped into the tub and gingerly sat down in it, favoring his side. It was a big tub, but still a tight fit for a man, sitting. He lifted his left arm, and screwed his head around to see the stitches along his side. They looked ugly enough, but not infected, not inflamed. He'd come out of that lightly enough, for a knife fight.

One of Chun's wives—a very fat one—came bustling into the room. She was chattering something in Chinese to an Indian girl following along behind her, lugging two buckets of steaming water. The Indian girl, short and stocky in a soaked missionary dress, didn't seem to understand Chinese, but Mrs. Chun kept it up at a great rate.

The girl set one of the buckets down and went to Lea's tub with the other. The water was still steaming, and looked way too hot to Lea. He was opening his mouth to say something about that when the Indian girl heaved the bucket up and poured the whole thing over on him.

"Jesus!" It was scalding hot. Lea hunched forward to lift his ass up as the hot water sloshed down into the tub. It burned the wound along his side. "Some *cold* water, for Christ's sake!"

No good. Mrs. Chun gestured to the Indian girl, and

the second bucket of hot water was dumped over his head. Lea cursed and struggled to his feet, lifting one foot and then the other out of that steaming water.

"Bath!" said Mrs. Chun, with considerable satisfaction, and she stumped over and handed Lea a chunk of brown lye soap.

When he walked out into the cool afternoon air, Lea felt pretty well. Clean, freshly shaved, and with every stitch he had on or was carrying under his arm washed and line-dried over the boiler firebox. It had cost three bits—really two. One extra to the Indian girl for going to get some cold water to pour in the tub.

Neither of the cuts seemed to have been harmed from the bath. They stung a little from the hot water, even more from the soap.

It was a touch more than cool outside though. He could tell it, fresh from the laundry shed. There was an edge to the air. A winter edge—still a way off, but coming down fast enough.

He walked past the stables, waved to one of the stableboys, a kid named Turley, and turned up the path to his cabin.

The moment he took that turn, he saw Larrabee. The old man, bold as brass, was up there waiting for him.

Larrabee had seen Lea, too, and raised his hand to greet him. The little old man, plump and rosy in a fine English tweet suit, his silver mutton-chop whiskers fluffed out as dandy as you please, was roosting at his ease on one of those dude shooting-sticks—a walking cane with a handle which folded out into a skimpy seat. Old man Larrabee leaned back, lounging at his ease as if he were in a parlor rocker. He smiled at Lea as he came up.

Lea didn't smile in return. He looked back over his shoulder instead. But there was no killer there.

"What do you want, Larrabee?" Lea said, and without waiting for an answer, walked past the old man, unlatched his cabin door, and went inside. He didn't intend to talk to a millionaire with laundry under his arm. He dumped the clean clothes on his cot, noticed that old Tocsen had moved out, bedroll and all —probably back to the grain barn, where he had a little hideout over the oats.

When he went back outside, the old man was still smiling, still lounging at his ease on that shooting stick.

"Won't you invite me in, Mr. Lea?" he said. He had a pleasant voice. It sounded younger than he was.

"No," Lea said.

The little man pursed his lips.

"Mr. Lea," he said. "Just about the first thing that I learned about business—and I learned it a very long time ago—was that it is *always* a mistake to lose one's temper. And *not,* mind you, only in business, but in all the contingencies of life. It is always unwise to lose one's temper." He glanced up at Lea, his bright blue eyes twinkling like anybody's merry grandfather. "Now," he said, "I have given you some very good advice in advance of our . . . *negotiations.* I wonder if you're wise enough to take advantage of it."

"You're mistaken, Larrabee, if you think I've lost my temper with you. I don't do that with people I intend to kill."

The twinkle went out of those bright blue eyes then.

"A number of men have threatened me, Mr. Lea. Men, I might add, in every way more formidable than a

151

wandering frontier rough. One way or another, each of those men have been . . . *disappointed.*" Then he smiled. "I see no reason to believe you an exception."

Lea smiled back at him. "Do you have anything else to say to me, Mr. Larrabee?"

"Why, yes. I do! We have exchanged—oh, I imagine you could call them threatening snorts, or roars, if you like." He chuckled. "Now, if you can bear it, I would like to do a little business."

"What kind?"

Larrabee rocked forward on the shooting stick, balancing himself neatly with the shiny black toes of his high-button boots. "Cash business, Mr. Lea, what else?"

"How much?"

The old man nodded. "Admirably direct. And so shall I be. Mr. Lea, you are a fairly formidable fellow. You have dispatched Mr. Budreau who, as I believe the term to be, was no *lily* himself. And previous to that you, with our brave Baron, dispatched three wandering outlaws. So you are a good man in a fight. A *very* good man." He rocked back, balancing himself nicely. "As a fighting man—particularly out here, so far from the intervention of more a civilized authority—you may present an obstacle worth, oh, say, five-thousand dollars, to remove." He glanced up at Lea. "Not impressed? Oh, dear. As it happens, you do have an additional value to the opposition, you might say. The French would call it *morale.* By your presence you *stiffen* the opposition. To remove that factor would, I suppose, be worth another five-thousand dollars."

He sat, smiling up at Lea, rocking gently back and forth. He had good balance for such an old man.

He was talking about a tremendous amount of

money. And that meant that there was, beyond any doubt, silver ore in the mountain at Little River. It meant that hundreds of millions of dollars were in the balance here—a god-awful way deep into Idaho mountains, at a hotel in the middle of nowhere.

And the ten-thousand dollars? Lea didn't doubt for a minute that Larrabee meant every word. It was more money than he'd ever had in one piece in his life. Money like that would *change* his life. He could go to Canada, or Mexico—anywhere—with that much money, and perhaps buy a small ranch, and stock it too. Or he could go east, where no one would ever know who he was, buy a house somewhere, buy into a business.

The old man was offering him a new life. If he could take it.

Larrabee knew the answer before Lea said a word.

"Oh, dear," he said. And he stood up and turned to fold the handle of his shooting stick. The top of his head didn't reach Lea's shoulder. "Oh, dear."

He stood for a moment, looking up at Lea.

"I'm sorry," he said. And he turned and walked away, leaning on the stick a little where the path was rough.

Lea stood looking after him, but the little old man didn't look back.

When he was a boy, Lea had once met Bill Longley in Texas. And, years later, he'd had lunch with Jesse James and his brother in New Orleans for the Sullivan fight. Meeting those men had been like meeting Larrabee. They were all very dangerous men, but it wasn't that that made them seem similar to Lea. It was their certainty. All of them had it. That air of having always won, of having always accomplished what they'd set out to do.

Winners all. And they'd ridden a sight of men down on their way.

Of course, Longley was dead now. Jesse too. No man was bigger than death.

That's why he had meant what he'd said about killing Larrabee, though he doubted the old man had taken him very seriously. It was not just that Larrabee *deserved* killing for having Edna O'Malley murdered. How the hell had that little girl dreamed she could blackmail a man like Larrabee?

There was no other way to beat him. No other way to save Gunstock, Abe and Sarah Bridge, because he'd surely murder them too; he'd have to. No other way to save Farris Lea either.

Let him keep breathing much longer, and that old man would eat them all alive.—This Shane, or whatever his name was, would only be the first. Soon, Larrabee would have an army in Gunstock. Hell, given enough time, he'd have the *U.S.* Army in Gunstock!

And, if the old man weren't bad enough, there was that damn Russian and those eight Cossack bullies of his, who'd be pleased to cut a man's throat—or whip him to death—if the Count were to raise his little finger.

So far, the Count and his men hadn't moved. But when they did all hell was going to break loose in Idaho!

Just maybe, Lea thought, I might have bitten off a plug too tough to chew. He went back inside the cabin to grease and sharpen the Arkansas toothpick, to clean and oil the Bisley Colt.

CHAPTER EIGHTEEN

In the morning Lea went up to the gun room for cartridges. It was just dawn and the lobby of the big hotel was deserted except for a few cleaning women finishing their night's work.

Then Lea went out to the stable, called for Turley, and finally got the dun out of his stall and saddled him himself.

He rode out toward the hotel ranch, two miles north of the main building. Halfway there, he pulled the dun up at the head of a small *barranca*. The gully was lined along its sides with scrub pine and red fern, but the uneven bottom of the draw was fairly clear. The ground ran some two-hundred yards straight out from the gully's head.

Lea left the dun tied at the head of the draw, took the Sharps and Greener down with him, and scrambled down the bank to the rutted dirt at the gully's base.

He left the firearms leaning against some brush, and climbed back up to the dun to untie a gunnysack full of peachcans from the cantle and lug it down into the draw.

He practiced all morning.

First, with the shotgun. He threw the cans for straight one-on-one shooting. Then he threw two at a time, swinging left and right to fire at both. When he stopped missing at that, he threw three cans at a time, and had to hustle to get the Greener reloaded and into position for his third shot. Stopping every now and then to let the shotgun cool, Lea kept at the three-can throw, wanting a good run of hitting all three before he quit. He finally got his run after two hours shooting.

He'd never be the hand with a scatter gun that the Count was, probably not as good as old Tocsen either. But he was as good as he was going to get, and that wasn't so bad as shotgun shooting went.

Then he picked up the Sharps and went to work. Two-hundred yards wasn't enough distance to really work the buffalo-gun out, so Lea worked on very fine shooting—on hitting the peach on the paper label, instead of just hitting the can.

He fired until his arm got tired, then he cut a hasty rest from a pine branch and used that. He did some good shooting with the Sharps—especially with the rest. He worked hard, and after more than an hour he was hitting the peach on the can labels eight out of ten shots at two-hundred yards. He knew other men who shot that well with a buffalo gun—though not many—but he considered that it was fair country shooting, for a *pistolero,* anyway.

And he'd for sure shot away a sight of cartridges. He'd have to tell Sarah to reorder.

The last few shots he took with the rifle, he fired as passing shots—fired from the hip at peach cans rolling along the sides of the gully. He hit one, missed three, but not by too much. There was no telling when he might have to use the big gun close up.

There was no telling anything about gunfighting, beforehand.

It was almost midday when he finally put the big Sharps down alongside the Greener. Lea'd skipped breakfast and was feeling more than a little hungry. That was all right—hungry was a good way to shoot.

Lea had brought both his Colts. He never wore more than one pistol—the damn things weighed too much—but he always carried a spare in his war bag. Any pistol, used hard, will shoot loose, and was a long way between good gunsmiths. His second gun was the image of the first. The same manufacture lot, in fact, so Lea could be sure the steel quality and the fit were as close to identical as the people in Hartford could make them. They were both Bisleys. He liked the shape of the grip; it sat back in his hand in a nice way.

He holstered one of the Colts, taking no particular care how it went into the leather, and commenced to stroll up and down the length of the gully, tossing peach cans this way and that, and drawing and shooting them.

He missed some, at first. Then he didn't.

He shot them straight on, and thrown high in the air, and he drew and shot them shied to the side, to rattle and bounce along the gully's sides. He pitched the cans behind him too, throwing them over his shoulder, and then underhand.

After a while he didn't miss any of them.

Lea almost never practiced with handguns. It didn't seem to make much difference to his shooting. He had known very fine shootists who practiced every day.

He'd heard that Hickok had done that—though the times he'd seen Hickok, that handsome pimp had usually been drunk as a skunk, and had stayed that way for nearly a week. So perhaps he didn't really practice as much as all that.

Still, Lea thought, here you are practicing now, all right. The great Buckskin Frank Leslie must be running just a mite scared.

He changed guns, and worked the other Bisley the way he had the first one, being careless as he pleased about how the pistol was holstered, as long as it was in there firm enough to stay without the riding-keeper strung under the hammer. Lea'd never liked fooling with the leather—soaking it for a shrink-fit on the piece, or polishing up the insides with tallow or graphite. It didn't seem much use, since almost always a gun fight happened when a man's holster was fresh soaked with rain or spilled beer, or dusted over with sawdust or trail dust, or rockhard with cold or rag-limp with Texas heat. And always when the damn holster was twisted around under a man's ass, and him sitting arms out of a captain's chair, half under a poker table, and often with some fat blonde hooker sitting in his lap to boot!

No use wasting much time on the leather.

Lea took some snapshots at pine branches—the four-dozen peach cans (courtesy of the Gunstock dump) by now were shot to such rags that he couldn't tell a hit from a miss; the rounds were as likely to sail right through without touching. He hit with his snapshots, and then tried to work on his draw.

That was no good, as it always was no good. The harder he worked, the slower he got. He had to relax,

158

back off trying and simply draw-an'-shoot.

Then, as if by magic, it was there again. The Colt seeming to jump up into his hand, the shot coming so fast. "Quick as bean farts," Doc had said about that draw. Holliday's own pull had been none too swift. It didn't have to be, as Doc said himself. "The poor bastards are scared stiff as pine boards, just standing up in front of me! It's the ones too drunk to be scared've got me worried!"

For the fun of it, Lea fired both Colts together, left and right, right and left. He blew a small pine in two fifty yards down the gully, twirled his guns like a kid, laughed, and put them away.

It took him a while to collect all the shot-up peach cans and put them back in the sack. Then he kicked the sack under some ferns and let it lie.

It took considerably longer to pick up his brass. There was a hell of a lot of it.

He finally had most of it up and jingling around inside his tucked-in shirt when he heard hoofbeats. He stood and listened, and heard them coming nearer.

One horse . . . coming fast.

Lea bent and kept picking up brass. He had to dig some of the cartridge cases out of the dirt where he'd stomped them in, marching up and down blazing away.

The horse came galloping on. It was pulled in and worked through the brush at the head of the gully.

Lea checked the loads in the second Bisley, slid the barrel of the .45 into his gunbelt on the left side, and stepped over to the near bank of the gully, under the cover of a shaggy little dwarf pine.

"Mr. Lea!" It was Sarah Bridge.

"Coming up!"

Lea went to pick up the Greener and Sharps, and then scrambled up through the brush to the head of the draw.

Sarah was standing in the scrub by a lathered horse. She was nearing a handsome blue riding dress, and carried a parrot-beak .38 in her belt. A nice little weapon.

Her face was white as milk.

"Mr. Lea. One of the gardener's men had seen you ride out this way. I . . . I rode after you and heard the firing—"

"I was practicing, Miss Bridge," Lea said. "Now, you'd better tell me what's the matter."

She stopped, and Lea saw her biting her lip hard. "Mr. Lea, *the Count is gone, and* his men!"

"Just now, you mean?"

She shook her head, her eyes filling with tears. "*No.* They rode out sometime last night."

"Hell's fire. Last *night?* I thought Drexel was watching them!"

Sarah Bridge looked sick, and well she might, Lea thought. She'd just received her father's death sentence.

"Leo *was* watching them! The Count caused a scene in the dining room last evening; he was drunk, and—"

"Pretending to be drunk."

She nodded miserably. "Yes. I'm afraid so."

"And he was put to bed in his suite, *drunk.* Right?"

She nodded.

"And Leo didn't bother to check on those Cossacks of his all night?"

She looked up, angry. "The stable boy was watching them!"

It made sense. The Russians had all bunked together in a lean-to out behind the stable. "And he saw nothing? Who was it?"

"It was Charlie Turley." She was glaring at Lea as if, somehow, this was all his fault. "And he's dead! We found him hanging from a *hook* in the tackroom." Her voice shook as she said it.

"All right," Lea said. "All right." He reached out and took her into his arms as naturally as can be. She came to him, and rested for a moment, leaning her cheek against the smooth, worn buckskin of his jacket. Lea felt her trembling against him.

"Crying?"

"No," she said. "No, I'm not."

Lea hugged her hard, then let her go.

"Lea . . ."

He turned away from her, picked up the Greener and Sharps, and kicked his way through the thick brush to the tethered dun.

He mounted and reined over to her, the rifle and shotgun balanced across his saddle-bow.

"Now, listen to me. Larrabee will figure your father dead for sure. That leaves you. Chances are he'll try for *you* sooner or later. Have you got a good woman who can stay with you—day and night?"

Sarah thought a moment. "Yes, I think so. There's a woman, Graciela, she helps de la Maine in the kitchen. She's an old friend of my father's."

"How tough is she? Can she handle a gun?"

"She's very tough, I think. She worked in saloons in the mining camps my father prospected at. I'm sure she can handle a gun. So can I!"

"All right. Get mounted. We'll talk as we go. Get her

161

out of that kitchen, give her a gun, and tell her what the hell is going on, if she doesn't know already. She's not to let you out of her sight! Day or night!"

Sarah swung up onto her mare, and Lea spurred the dun out of the scrub into the long grass, headed back up the valley to the hotel. She urged the mare up alongside him, and they rode in silence for a moment.

"And be careful of your food. You and this woman eat in the kitchen. De la Maine's no fool. He'll cook it *and* serve it to you."

"Yes. I'll do that."

"Now, when did the Russians ride out?"

"Sometime after midnight."

"Christ." Lea spurred the dun into a gallop, and Sarah urged her mare after him.

They rode together, running the horses hard, tracking side by side through the tall yellow grass. The wind was cold in their faces.

They rode into the stable yard, and Lea swung down from the dun while it was still pacing.

"Go up and ask the Baron if I can borrow that damned stallion of his! I'll need more speed than my old friend can give me." He stroked the dun's flank for a moment, then led him into the stalls.

With the dun in his box, Lea trotted acorss the stableyard and up the path to his cabin. He pushed through the door, glanced around for Tocsen. The old man wasn't there. No saying he'd want in on this either. It was white man's business, after all.

Lea scooped up his bedroll, boxes of cartridges—his, not the hotel's—shoved his old sheepskin jacket, an extra pair of wool socks and his long-johns into his saddlebags.

Then he was out of the cabin, heading back toward the stables at a run. *After midnight,* he thought. It's a hell of a head start. A full day's start.

When he got to the stable, Sarah had already come down again. The Baron was with her, puffing from the stairs, his right arm in a sling. Toby Easterby was with him.

"So, Lea, you need my bad-behaved stud? I think you need help too? No? I come!"

The old squarehead was showing up all right.

"I'm coming along also, Mr. Lea."

"No," Lea said, "neither of you. It's not your business. No need for either of you to get killed in it. What you *can* do is keep an eye on Sarah. Watch out for her."

The old German blustered about that for a moment, but Toby Easterby nodded and said: "Very well, Mr. Lea. I promise you we'll take good care of Miss Bridge. I understand that Mr. Larrabee is the villain in the piece?"

"And those Russians!" The Baron went stamping back into the stalls to get the stud out. They heard him bellow for the stable-boy, then a sudden, embarrassed silence, as he remembered the boy's death.

"Take some of the hands, then, Lea!" Sarah said.

"Your father took the best half-dozen gun-hands he had, Sarah. What's left are pure cowpokes, not worth much in a gunfight. That's if Larrabee hasn't already got to one or two of them with some cash money . . ." Lea shook his head. "I'd better leave them be."

They heard a clatter of hooves as the Baron, handicapped by his slung arm, led the big stallion out. The big bay rolled his eyes and pranced, full of grain. *Just the way I need the big bastard, too,* Lea thought.

163

The Baron held the stud while Lea and Easterby got him saddled and bridled, and Lea lashed the saddlebags and rifle-boot on him.

Then Lea swung up.

The big bay lurched and shied into a buck, but Lea roweled his sides and leaned forward to hit the horse between the ears with his fist. The stud snorted and danced across the cobbles, but he didn't throw another buck.

"Goot!" the Baron called. "Dat's how you ride him!"

"Good luck, old man!"

"Lea."

Lea tipped his Stetson to them, spurred the stallion, and rode away.

CHAPTER NINETEEN

The big bay was a fast one, no doubt about that. And he had as many bad manners as the old Baron had himself. He'd break stride, buck, and shy at nothing but a windblown leaf.

Lea gathered him in every time, spurred him, hit him when he had to, and after more than two hours on the road, had the stud leveled out and running smooth.

The stallion was as strong as an ox, once he settled down. And fast. Maybe even as fast as the dun had been in its prime.

And the horse was going to have to be. Because Lea intended to drive it straight toward Little River, hitting the ridges all the way.

There was no way to catch the Russians in a stern chase; they were well mounted and they'd too damn much of a start. The most Lea could hope for was to shortcut, and come up on their ambush—because they'd sure as hell set one to catch Abe and his men riding back from that railroad cut.

As he rode, Lea laid the country out in his mind,

looking for a dead-sure place for a bushwhacking.

It depended on how far Abe had ridden back before the Russians met him. If he was a full day out of Little River, the Count's best chance would be in the wooded hills south of Smokey. If Abe hadn't gotten that far the Russians might catch him at Fork Creek.

Fork Creek was the place Lea would have picked. That little stream ran through a steep, rough valley no more that a pistol shot across. It would be turkey-shooting for the Cossack's carbines.

Lea knew Abe had taken fair-enough men with him. Abe wouldn't have hired them in the first place if they weren't first-class cowhands. The beef from Gunstock's ranch wasn't raised for the hotel alone. Gunstock beef was driven and shipped clear to Chicago. No question of Abe's men being good with cows.

And the six he'd taken with him must be able to handle guns at least well enough to pass for fighting men. Lea'd known plenty of cowpokes who liked a fight—and even a few who really knew how. Most working cowboys never had the time, or the application, to get really fine with a gun. Still, likely they'd give a good account of themselves—if the Count was foolish enough to give them a fair chance.

The Count hadn't struck Lea as that kind of a fool.

No; he'd lay his Cossacks off in an ambush of some kind, and they'd knock down Abe's men—and old Abe —just as fast as they could. Abe and six cowboys together were almost fair odds against the Count and his eight Cossacks, even with the Cossacks being professional fighting men. The odds would be *too* fair for the Count.

One way or another, the little black-eyed nobleman

would see those odds knocked down.

But if Lea could ride up on the Russians in time. One more gun, a professional gun, might make the difference.

Lea spurred the big bay out across a grassy flat, running the stallion full-out. Soon enough, they'd be up on the ridges, in the tanglefoot and shale slides. There wouldn't be much galloping up there.

By late afternoon, Lea was riding the ridges south toward Little River. The big stud was going steady as a steam engine.

The weather was holding, as it had held for days, clear, sunny, and getting colder. As the bay climbed the hills, Lea reached back and broke his sheepskin out of the saddlebags. The wind had an edge to it.

He thought about the Count as he rode, and he thought about the Cossacks too.

They were professionals, and they were used to big, rough, wild country. They were used to riding hard. They had military discipline, and they did what they were told. They were frontiersmen; they had been raised to fight Tartars as savage and elusive an enemy as any Comanche.

These particular men were armed with Nagent revolvers and Russian carbines—and sabers. And all this was pure bad news.

But *they* had weaknesses too.

Lea figured they might be a little lost, should something happen to that fine Count of theirs. Their sergeant—if that's what he was—that giant Grigori, didn't strike Lea as being particularly bright. Likely he wouldn't be too handy a commander with the Count dead. And sure as hell none of the rest of them seemed like officer material.

No. The way to handle those *hombres* was to surprise them—and to get a bullet into the Count!

Could be that the Cossacks might be surprised, too, at the fight the cowboys would put up. From what Lea'd heard, Cossacks weren't too used to ordinary citizens coming back at them in a fight.

And there was the rub. Because what *he* knew, the Count knew better. And that was why the Count would be doing the surprising, at Fork Creek or wherever he could, and why he was sure as hell going to bushwhack those cowboys down before they could come back hard at his men.

Lea swung off the bay, and led him over a shattered stretch of scree. The big stallion didn't seem to be tiring, but the weight off his back for a mile or two would give him a breather.

Lea stumped along through the rattling shale, the bay following quietly on a rein lead.

Lea hadn't seen any tracks. Not that they would have bothered to brush them out. Why should they? He knew where they were going, and he knew how they'd get there. They would have ridden at a good speed, but not as fast as they could, not as fast as he was taking the stallion. And they would have headed straight south, straight for Little River. Probably by map. In doing that, they would have ridden up and down half a dozen steep hills and ridges.

Far out to the west, the long great line of the Bitteroots marched down from the north. The snow on their peaks glittered in the early evening light. The snow shone farther down the jagged granite falls and buttresses than it had only a week before. Winter was blowing down from the peaks and high passes.

Lea felt it in the wind that hissed softly through rough grass along the ridge. It stung his face and his hands. He walked along a little farther, another quarter mile or so, looking always out to the south, looking for a smudge of smoke that might mean the Cossacks had stopped to make a fire for their tea, or had hunted as they rode, and stopped to stick-broil a haunch of venison.

There was nothing. Lea had not really expected it. The Russians probably did not think he'd be coming after them. It would be the Shoshones they'd be wary of. It was unlikely, though, that the Indians, whipped to a bone by the cavalry in the past few years, would want to attack a party of nine well-armed men.

After walking a last, bad stretch of shale, Lea swung up into the saddle again, picked up the big bay's head from nibbling at stray moss flowers, and spurred the stallion into a lope.

He would run the big horse until dark. At night it would be too dark to ride. The high clouds coming down on the wind would shade out the moonlight. After sunset, when darkness fell, he and the Russians both would have to step down to sleep until dawn.

Two hours after daybreak the Russians would meet Abe Bridge at Fork Creek or beyond. And, if it killed him and his horse, Lea would be there too.

In a high, saddleback dip, fifteen miles or so from the Creek, Lea staked the stallion out, hobbled him for good measure, and then rolled himself into his blankets to sleep. It was dark by then, like the inside of a stovepipe hat. The wind was blowing stronger from the north.

He decided he was a damn fool, rooted with his shoulder for some comfort as he lay, and went slowly to sleep, waking a little now and then when the wind gusted harder, or stopped.

He dreamed toward waking, and only for a while. He dreamed he was a boy again, standing in the hot white dust of the road, watching his father ride off to fight in the war. His brother was riding off too.

Even in the dream, Frank knew that was wrong. They hadn't gone together; his father had gone first, and been killed. Then his brother had gone, and been killed, too. But that had taken years, and they'd never gone away together like that.

He felt how hot the road dust was under his bare feet, and he heard his mother saying something.

His father didn't turn around to wave, but his brother did. Frank saw his face as plain as day against the bright green of the sycamores along the road.

"Wave goodbye," his mother said.

Lea woke with a grunt. He turned over and looked up into a dead black sky.

He sat up, looking to the east. There, along the distant hills, a narrow ribbon of gray edged the far horizon. The wind had died; the air was still and cold as cold water. The bay stallion bulked in the darkness, shifting a little. It was time to move out.

Lea rolled out of the soogins, stood in the darkness and stretched, working the stiffness out of his muscles and joints. His side hurt him. He reached down, picked up his gun belt, and strapped it on. Then he took a few strides out to the edge of the ridge, unbuttoned his trousers and pissed a stream out into the night. Hunger was on him. The stallion would be hungry, too, wanting grain.

Lea went to the horse, knelt to unhobble him, pulled the screw-stake out, and saddled and bridled him. The bay fought the cold bit, clenching his teeth against it, but Lea held his ear and tapped the bit against those big yellow teeth, dim in the darkness, till the horse took it.

Then he swung up into the saddle, looked back to see the dawn coming down the ridge, and kicked the bay into a trot.

Lea dug in his sheepskin pocket for a strip of jerky, chewed it down, then chased it with a long drink of water. It tasted of metal, and was cold enough to hurt his teeth.

"Cold bit, cold water," he said to the stallion, wondering if a German horse understood English.

When it grew light enough, he spurred the bay into a gallop.

At twenty minutes to eleven o'clock, by his watch, Lea rode the sweating bay along the last slope of the southern ridge. Half a mile to the west was the Fork Creek ford.

The stallion was lathered from the long run, and foam fell from the bridle chain, but he still went well, and was breathing as deeply as a sleeping child.

"Good horse," Lea said to him, and stroked it along the neck. "You're a beauty. Yes you are."

They were out of the shale, and the stallion's hooves thudded along the rough turf. To the right, the ridge fell away in a steep slope, too steep to run the bay down safely. That slope leveled out, two-hundred feet below, into a broad valley full of thick, high, yellow grass—buffalo and gamma and wild wheat.

171

Out there in the valley Lea saw the first sign the Russians had left. A narrow beaten track cutting through the the high grass to the west. It was interesting to see; the Cossacks traveled like Indians, in single file.

Lea kicked the bay into a lunging gallop, and he strained his eyes toward Fork Creek.

CHAPTER TWENTY

He rode along the ridge for another few hundred yards, the bright late-morning sunlight stretching his shadow ahead of them as they went. A wind was up, gusting and shifting over the ridge.

Then he saw Abe Bridge and his cowhands.

They were riding toward him, loping, bunched and alert, their rifles across their saddle-bows, up from the narrow end of the valley, away from Fork Creek.

There were seven of them. Old Abe and his half dozen. By the look of them, even at a considerable distance, they had been expecting trouble back at the ford.

And there hadn't been any. The Russians hadn't tried for them. And damned if Lea could understand why.

Unless the ford at the creek was too obvious. Abe looked to have been ready for trouble there.

Lea pulled the sweating stallion down to a walk, and lifted the big Sharps out of its scabbard. He'd wait till Abe was closer, then give him a warning shot and ride down to join him. If the Russians had made no trouble here, they damn well would make trouble somewhere else—maybe over at Smokey.

The wind blew across the ridge, and swept down into the narrowing valley. Lea watched as it combed through the thick grass there. Grass as high as a horse's shoulder.

It combed the grass back in long surging rows of yellow and green.

That's where Lea saw the Cossacks.

They'd laid their horses down in a great half-circle in the grass. The Cossacks lay beside them, their carbines in their hands. Lea saw them here and there, then lost sight of them as the restless wind blew the grass in billows back and forth.

He saw them from the ridge, lookig down, but Abe and his cowhands would see nothing. They were already riding into that great half-circle.

Lea raised the Sharps and fired.

The sound boomed across the valley. Abe and his men looked up to see Lea, outlined on the ridge above, pointing furiously down into the valley before them.

Abe Bridge was nobody's fool. It took him just a moment to recognize Lea, another moment to realize what he was warning them.

He was the least bit too late. They were just within the circle.

From the ridge, Lea saw the Cossacks and Orloff. He recognized the Count leaping up, mounting his horse. He saw them rise out of the buffalo grass and fire in one long rolling volley into the cowhands they almost surrounded.

Lea saw three of the cowboys go down hard. He reloaded the Sharps, stood in the stirrups, and tried a shot at the Count. Tried, and lost him in the drifting gunsmoke. Then he bucketed the Sharps, turned the stallion's head to the pitch of the slope, and spurred him down toward the valley below.

The side of the ridge fell away almost vertically. The stallion leaped out and down, slid, scrambled, and found his feet. It was fall or gallop down. The big bay galloped.

Lea lay back against the cantle, yanking at the straps to loose the Greener as they went. He expected the stallion to fall, and tried to shake his boots loose in the stirrups so he could kick his way clear when they went down.

The bay's tail whipped at his face as he lay back almost to the horse's rump. The Greener finally came free, and he had it in his right hand. He couldn't keep the reins; the stallion's head was too far down. He saw above him the tilting slope of the ridge; below, the narrow valley was exploding in gunfire, hazed by gunsmoke.

The stallion slipped. Lea felt his guts twist inside him as the horse began to fall. Then, with a crack of hoof on stone, a slamming blow up against Lea's back, the bay recovered.

When the stallion struck level ground, the high, hissing foliage of the grass, the jolt almost slung Lea away and out of the saddle. He almost lost the shotgun as well. Lea held on—more by luck than skill—and kept the Greener too. He heaved himself upright in the saddle, dug his boots deeper into the stirrups, and spurred the big bay on, thundering through the high grass, into the fight.

The cowboys had done all right. Three of them were

down and dead, and one of those still in the saddle hurt badly and swaying as he rode. Still, Abe was leading the remnants straight at the Cossack line in a charge.

It was the only chance they had.

As he cut across the valley toward the fight, Lea saw Abe riding down on one of the Russians, blazing away at the man with a pistol. The Cossack, up and mounted, sat his horse dead-still and sighted the old man with his carbine resting over his arm as if he were hunting. It was not the way to work against Abe Bridge.

Lea saw the old man as he bore down, the four cowhands riding hard behind him, revolvers smoking. Lea saw Abe fire twice, three, four times at the Cossack before him. And the Russian sagged in the saddle. The carbine swung out to the side as the Cossack leaned down from his horse, then slipped and fell from it.

Abe and his men came riding through.

Just as they did, another Russian, riding almost parallel to their ambush line, snap-shot with his Winchester and knocked Abe Bridge out of the saddle.

Lea hauled on the rein to bring the stallion over—he'd have to teach this brute neck-reining for sure, he thought—and raised the Greener as he and the Cossack galloped along for a moment, side by side across fifty feet of grass.

The Russian turned and saw Lea, then levered his carbine. He was a tall, black-bearded man with a bony face.

Lea shot him center with the right barrel of the Greener.

He saw the Cossack flinch, his long flap-tailed black coat fly out as the buckshot struck him. He fell back off of his running horse, hung from a stirrup for a moment,

176

squealing in agony, and then dropped free.

Lea saw one of the cowhands fire down with his Peacemaker at a Cossack shooting from the grass. The Cossack fell sideways, kicking.

There was a volley of Winchester rounds, and one of the cowhands riding toward Lea, shouting something, was knocked out of the saddle. His horse was shot too. It stumbled and went down.

A Cossack fired at Lea from the grass. He heard the bullet in the air past his head.

Lea turned to find him, but the man had ducked away.

He turned in the saddle again, and saw a Russian riding down on him. The Cossack had a pistol in his hand. Lea saw that it was the tall, blond man who'd grinned at him on the kitchen path.

Lea spun the stallion, and fell to the side to lie along the horse's neck as the blond man shot at him. Then, Lea fired the left barrel of the Greener from under the horse's neck.

The charge hit the blond man in his face. One of his eyes hung dangling as he rode past.

Lea turned the bay again, and drove him back into the fight, looking for the Count.

As he rode in through a cloud of gunsmoke, he saw two Cossacks hacking at a wounded cowhand with their sabers. It was Folliard. The old ranny fired a shot at one of them, but missed. Folliard was slumped in the saddle, trotting along with bright blood running down his horse's side. He'd been shot in the first volley, and was bleeding to death.

The two Cossacks, wheeling away when he fired the wild shot, turned back after him now. They rode down on him and hit him with their sabers again, cutting his head, chopping at his arms. The old cowhand was dead. One of the Cossacks leaned out of his saddle, laughing, and drove his saber into the cowboy's back as he lay, doubled across his horse's saddle-bow.

Lea rode to them. The nearest Cossack turned to call to him, thinking him a Russian. Lea drew and shot him twice through the belly.

The other man pulled his saber free, wheeled his horse, and spurred it at Lea, yelling. Lea took care with this man, and aimed and shot him through the right shoulder. The Cossack dropped his saber and fell back across his horse's haunch, but the horse kept running.

As it passed Lea on the run, he leaned out and shot the Cossack again just above the hips, so the bullet would go through his bowels.

A round hit Lea then, fired from somewhere behind him. It struck him lightly just under his left arm from front to back, and knocked him half out of the saddle.

A Cossack came riding past him through the smoke, but didn't seem to see Lea, and went on his way.

Someone shot at Lea again. The bullet blew his saddle horn away with a crack. He spurred the stallion and saw a Russian running through the grass toward him. It was that big sergeant, Grigori.

Where in hell was the *Count?*

The giant Cossack stopped running, and stood to take better aim. Lea turned in the saddle to shoot him, and a cowhand jumped out of the grass and grappled with the Russian. It spoiled Lea's shot.

It was Tiny Morgan, already shot once, but paying it no heed.

The two huge men grappled and butted like bulls.

Lea kicked the stallion away through the grass and gunsmoke, looking for the little black-eyed Count. His side hurt as he rode, but whether it was the gunshot or the old wound opening up, he didn't know.

He rode out into the open, and saw the Count sitting on a fine roan horse, talking to two of his men, and waving his hand. He looked angry. Lea thought it must be because the fight had cost him more than he'd figured on.

The big bay was almost done. Lea felt him stagger under him, and wondered if he'd been hurt in the shooting.

One of the Russians turned and saw him. He saw the Count turn and look at him too, and shake his head. It looked as though he was smiling.

The three Russians turned as one and came at him. The Count held a pistol in his hand; the other two began to fire their Winchesters. The stallion squealed as a round burned his side, and he heaved and bucked to the right. Lea tried to keep his seat, but his left side hurt terribly and took away his strength.

The stallion bucked again, and Lea was off, pitching out into the high grass, the Bisley Colt clutched in his hand.

He hit hard, rolled, and heard the hoofbeats coming.

He scrambled to his feet, yelling from the pain along his side, and dove deeper into the grass.

The hoofbeats drove in after him. When he stopped running and turned, he saw a Cossack with bright blue eyes leaning from the saddle to shoot at him with a carbine.

Lea shot the man and saw him flinch, but then the Cossack lifted the carbine to sight again. Lea shot him through the forehead just as he fired and saw, when the man fell, that the back of his head was broken open. Lea wasn't hit. He didn't know how the man had missed him. The other Cossack shot at Lea, and he fell and rolled along the ground to duck the shot. The man rode close and fired again. Lea came to his knees and started to shoot back. Then he remembered the Colt was empty.

The Cossack saw that, and so did the Count. Lea heard the Count laugh and say something in Russian.

The Cossack pulled in his horse, and for a moment, nobody did anything. Lea thought of reloading, but the Cossack was sitting on his horse just a little way away, watching him, and there would be no time. Lea wished to God he'd put his second Colt in his belt, but he hadn't. It was with the stallion.

The Count called out something, and Lea heard a sliding sound. He looked and saw that the Cossack had drawn his saber. The Russian wheeled his horse and came at Lea very fast.

Lea ran away into the tall grass as fast as he could, limping from the pain in his side, and gasping for breath. He ran as fast as he had ever run in his life, and the hoofbeats ran behind him. He heard the Count laughing.

The Cossack was on him very suddenly; he must have seen the grass moving where Lea ran, and come riding straight to him. Lea felt the hoofbeats in the ground, heard the grass hissing to his right, looked over his shoulder and saw the bulk of the horse and the man on him, and a sun-bright curve of steel.

He stopped in his tracks, threw himself back, and rolled under the horse's hooves.

The blade hummed down in a flash of light and cut his coat-sleeve and his arm, though he didn't feel it. Then he was up on his feet with his side on fire and running the other way.

The Cossack must have wheeled his horse and cut at him backhand. Lea heard the man grunt, and felt the whiffle of the blade past the back of his neck.

Lea heard the Count laughing again. He ran a little way, stopped, and turned as the Cossack came after him. The Cossack had a wide, pockmarked face, and he looked tired and angry. He carried the saber up resting over his shoulder, and he rode down on Lea at a gallop.

Lea took a step to the left to set himself better in the tangle of tall grass, bent down and pulled the Arkansas toothpick from his right boot. He leaned back and wound up, and threw the knife overhand as if he were pitching in a baseball game.

He threw it as hard as he could, then ducked and rolled into the grass to his right. It did not seem that he would be able to get up again, no matter what happened.

He heard the Cossack grunt as he rode in, and he thought he saw him swing the saber. Then he thought he'd thrown it, because the sword came flying, spinning end over end, and fell into the grass.

Then Lea saw that the Cossack had ridden past. His horse was trotting. Then it stopped and bent its head to graze.

The Cossack sat in his saddle, bent forward, for a moment. Then he swung his leg over to dismount, slid down to the ground, and then knelt down. When he did that, Lea saw the hilt of the knife sticking out of his chest, on the left side.

The Count called, and the man muttered something in Russian. Then he slowly lay back in the grass with his eyes open. Blood had soaked his black uniform.

Lea heard the Count cursing, and heard the hoofbeats coming toward him. He thought of getting up, and getting the saber the man had dropped. He could try with that.

It seemed like too much trouble.

CHAPTER TWENTY-ONE

Lea watched the Count ride to where the Cossack was sitting, dying with the knife in his chest.

The Count looked down at the man for a moment, but he didn't say anything. Lea thought of reloading the Colt, but he didn't know where it was. He'd dropped it while he was running. He got up and stood anyway.

The Count turned his horse, and rode over to Lea. He had a handsome, nickle-plated revolver in his hand.

The Count sat his big roan, looking down at Lea. The Cossack had looked tired, but the little Count didn't. He looked fresh as a daisy. His riding clothes were clean, and Lea could see a reflection of the grass in the gleaming polish of his right boot. His black eyes were bright as a child's.

"What an afternoon," he said. He looked down at Lea and pursed his lips. "Those men of Bridge's fought well . . . really well." He turned and looked out over the valley. "I don't see Grigori." He sighed. "I assumed my Grigori would live forever."

The Count glanced down at Lea, and shifted in the

saddle. Lea heard the leather creak.

"They were a surprise, those men." He smiled. "But not such a surprise as you, Mr. Lea. How on earth did you get here so quickly?"

Lea cleared his throat. "I rode the ridge south."

"Ah," the Count said. "I see. I thought of doing that, but I didn't care to outline my men there for any of your red savages to observe. Perhaps I was too cautious." He cocked the pistol.

"I wonder . . ." he said. "Are you . . . were you an army officer, perhaps? You are certainly an accomplished fighting man!"

"No," Lea said. "I'm a gunman. And I've been a pimp, and I've owned a ranch." Let the stuck-up son-of-a-bitch chew on that.

The Count laughed. "I see. A rogue! And a professional." He lifted the revolver and aimed it off-hand at Lea's head. "Well," the Count said, "as something of a rogue myself, I wish you farewell."

He looked surprised all of a sudden—astonished—as if he'd just realized something. And he screamed a short sharp scream like a girl's when she sees a rat on the kitchen floor.

He twisted in the saddle and the revolver went off. He grabbed at something at the small of his back.

Lea saw the polished wood and bright yellow fletching of a Shoshone arrow. The Count broke the shaft as he tried to pull it away. Inside him, the iron barb held fast.

Then another arrow came soaring through the air and into the Count's side. That one went in deep, almost to the feathers. Lea looked to see if the head had come poking out of him on the other side, but it hadn't.

184

The Count had dropped his revolver. He grabbed the fletching of the second arrow and tugged at it. And he looked down at Lea as if he was going to ask for help. The third arrow came and hit him higher. It snapped into the side of his chest, and Lea could see that the head of it must be deep into his lungs. It was a killing shot.

The Count stopped pulling at the arrow shafts. He threw back his head and screamed. The roan began to side-step, nervous at the noise. After a moment, the Count stopped screaming and tried to catch his breath, but he couldn't. He began to drown in his blood. Lea heard him gulping, gargling as he tried to breath. He was belching blood, and the smell made his horse shy and trot away with him.

Lea watched as the nervous roan trotted away, taking the Count with it. He saw the Russian, still sitting upright in the saddle, tearing with his hands at his mouth, his throat, throwing his head far, far back, trying to breath. His hands were red as paint.

"Where Greener?" Tocsen said, walking through the grass. The old man looked mighty sore. "You take."

Lea sat down to have a rest.

Tocsen stood in front of him and shook his bow angrily. He was mighty sore. "When we go," he said. "*I* take Greener. Every time!"

Tocsen searched through the grass for the shotgun. When he found it, and had walked down Lea's skittish bay for the shells to reload it, he was then ready to help Lea with Tiny Morgan. Morgan was the only Gunstock man alive, and he'd been bled out to a fare-the-well. Lea found him with the big Cossack, Grigori. The Cossack's neck was broken, and his head had been turned all the

185

way around.

He should never have whipped a horse in Tiny's stable.

Abe Bridge was dead. That single carbine shot had taken him through the heart.

The other Gunstock hands were dead as well. Two of them had been wounded by gunfire, then finished with sabers.

Six of the Cossacks were dead, and the last two—one of them was one that Lea'd shot in the belly—were bad hurt and dying. Tocsen cut their throats. Then he scalped the other six. Lea assumed the old man intended to claim the bunch should another Shoshone ever inquire about it.

Lea had lost sight of the Count. But Tocsen had an eye for the roan. He found the horse grazing all the way back by Fork Creek, and found the Count lying there beside him. He'd ridden all that way, dead. Tocsen scalped him, then cut off his nose to make him look silly on the other side.

That night, they camped a little farther up the valley. They heated the barrel of one of the Nagent pistols and burned Tiny Morgan's leg wound closed. They had gathered the horses that were alive and not wounded. They'd shot the others. It turned out there were Lea's bay, the Count's roan, two Gunstock ponies, and six Cossack horses in fine shape.

Lea figured the Cossack horses to be Tiny Morgan's to keep—if he lived.

They sat in a circle stomped clear of grass around a bright little fire and ate horse steak. Tocsen chewed some up the way the squaws did for children and old people, and Tiny ate that without a murmur. The big man had fits of crying over killing the Russian. That seemed to bother him more than having the gunshot wound burned closed.

Lea thought he was going to have to have that done for him, too. But Tocsen looked at the wound under his arm, and said no. His side was all bruised, black and purple and swollen under the stitches. No question he'd done himself harm riding, *and* in the fight. Tocsen washed the wound under his arm. He found some liquor in a Russian's canteen and poured that over it. It hurt bad enough to make Lea sick. He ate his steaks anyway, and drank a great deal of cold water from Fork Creek.

It was a cold, still night. Lea felt full of meat and cold water, and he felt a little sick. He said goodnight to Tiny Morgan, and patted the big man on the shoulder and told him he'd been very brave. Then he told Tocsen to take the damn Greener and keep it. He'd pay the hotel the price.

Then he lay down by the fire and rolled himself into his blankets. He wondered if he'd injured his side so much that it would never heal. He also wondered how to tell Sarah Bridge that her father had been killed under his eye. Under his gun. Because he'd been a little slow in figuring, and not looked as soon and as sharp as he should.

In the morning he was the first up. He was stiff as a pine board. His side and the gunshot wound under his arm hurt like boils. In spite of that, Lea felt very well. He took deep breaths of cold morning air, and he stood away from camp, pissed, and watched the gray dawn turning to sunrise in the east. Then he went out to the bodies.

No coyotes had come to them in the night. The buzzards would lead those into the valley today. Lea went to a dead Cossack first and got his Arkansas toothpick back. Then he walked to all the cowhand corpses and went through their pockets for anything that might tell of a family, anything they might like to have as a keepsake of these men. There wasn't much.

Old Folliard had a son in prison in New Mexico. Seemed to have been mixed up with Bill Bonney out there. A man named O'Reilly had a sister in Sioux City, a laundress at an Army post. A man named Peterson had been thinking of going home to farm. Then Lea collected the guns.

He couldn't find his own Colt. It was lost somewhere in there, buried out of sight in the high grass. He was glad he had the other Bisley in his saddlebag.

Finally, he went to Abe's body.

The old man lay stretched on his back, yawning, as if he were just waking from a nap on some country picnic.

Lea found a fine watch on him; "From Lil—With Love" was engraved inside the cover. And he found a bill from Boise Liquor and Sundries Supply, and a big bill from a freight outfit in Colorado.

Lea took Abe's wallet, but didn't open it, and took his fine spotted silk scarf as well. It wasn't damaged, and there was no blood on it. It was something Sarah might want to have.

Later in the morning, Lea and Tocsen dug a shallow grave, wrapped Abe Bridge in a blanket and put him into it. Then they went back to camp, hoisted Tiny Morgan up onto one of the Cossack horses, and rode away.

They'd ride the ridge back, the way Lea had come down from Gunstock. Tiny's leg and Lea's side would hold out better riding on the level rather than hauling up and down across a dozen ridges. They'd ride the same ridge Lea had—but slower. It was two full days to Gunstock.

Lea led, riding one of the Gunstock ponies. The Baron's bay needed at least another day's rest. Tiny Morgan followed. And Tocsen, muttering and singing to himself, the Greener across his saddle-bow, brought up the rear. Tocsen was riding the Count's tall roan and leading his paint pony behind him. He finished one song and started another.

By the next day, Lea was feeling better, and so was Tiny's leg. The leg was stiff, but didn't hurt so much.

They had horse steak again for breakfast. The meat tasted all right, but was giving them all the trots. Poetic justice, Lea said, but old Tocsen didn't understand jokes when they were told in English, and Tiny wasn't smart enough to understand it, although he laughed anyway when he saw that Lea would like that.

The Cossack horses gave them some trouble, too. They weren't used to being led, and started out the first day pushing and kicking to be first on trail. Tiny finally found the natural leader, a mean black gelding. When he was put up in front, the rest of the string quieted down.

Tocsen, though, was disappointed with Count Orloff's tall roan. The roan was too nervous for him, and it was always wanting to do this or that, shy here or start there. The old Shoshone wasn't used to blood horses, and he didn't like them. He beat the roan, and that just made him worse.

"Pet him," Lea said. "Make him like you, and he'll do what you want."

Making a horse *like* him was not in Tocsen's usual line. It was not in any Shoshone's usual line. It might be something that the Nez Percé did. And if that is what their spirits urged on them, he supposed they had no voice in the matter.

Tocsen got down off his high horse by noon on the second day's traveling, and climbed aboard his shambling little pinto. There had never been any question of affection between those two, but there was considerable respect on both sides.

On the morning of the third day they saw the high slate roof shining wet in the sun. It was a sight to see.

A rain shower had swept down the valley as they rode into it, and a long, fading rainbow arched out from High Pass at the valley's western edge.

Tiny was very excited, and pointed it out. He'd been told about the pot of gold as a child, and people had amused themselves with him lately, by telling him it was true. He told Lea that he'd gone to look for the gold twice, to buy a set of harnesses with bells on it, and had probably just missed finding it.

Lea didn't know what to say to the big man at first— but in order to keep him from galloping off up the valley after his pot of gold, finally said that indeed there had once *been* gold at the end of every rainbow. But that it had been taken away lately, so that people would be content to enjoy the rainbow's prettiness, rather than being greedy.

The big man was struck by this, and thought about it. He finally nodded and rode along content.

Lea worried about Tiny as if the giant were a child.

190

He decided it came from not having real children of his own to raise.

For his part, Tocsen acted with more respect toward Tiny Morgan than he did to Lea. He thought the big man had a spirit in his head.

They rode along the ranch boundary, past the dairy buildings, and into the west pastures. There were Jerseys in one of the fenced fields, and two teams of Belgian geldings in the other.

Then they rode past the laundry, the kitchen gardens, and into the stableyard. A party of guests were riding out as they rode in, clattering over the cobbles. It was a group of young men and women, some of them in hunting pinks. The only foxes around Gunstock were grays. They were no good to hunt, since they simply ran to the nearest slanting tree, and climbed it. Coyotes were good coursing though, and Gunstock made a considerable fuss about its hounds and rough-country coyote hunting.

The wrangler, Davies, was taking this bunch out, riding down to the kennels to pick up Chasen and the pack.

Davies stared at Lea as he rode by, but he didn't say anything.

They pulled up at the stable, and Tiny swung down stiffly to take their horses. Lea told him that Edwards would be coming out to look at his leg, and Tiny nodded, smiling. Lea had told him that Charlie Turley was dead, but as Tiny led the horses in, Lea heard him calling to the boy. He'd forgotten.

Tocsen walked away toward the cabin, muttering, the Greener over his shoulder, his rawhide sack dragging along the cobbles.

191

Lea walked across the stableyard to the path through the kitchen gardens. It seemed a very long walk to take. He wished to God it was longer.

De la Maine had heard he was back. He saw the massive Frenchman standing at the top of the steps to the kitchen door. Some halfbreed girls were peeping out behind him.

De la Maine looked into Lea's eyes as he came up the path, then made a face and shook his head sadly.

When Lea came up the steps, the big Frenchman sighed and shook his hand. "I will miss that so-loud Monsieur Bridge," he said. "*La petite* has heard you are here. She is coming down to the kitchens now."

Lea stood in the doorway, with nothing to say.

CHAPTER TWENTY-TWO

Sarah came into the kitchen, looked to the door and saw him standing there. She pushed her way through the crowd of kitchen help, all standing in the passageway, murmuring, turning to look at her as she strode past them. A stocky, black-haired woman was walking behind her.

"Lea."

He shoved his way through to her, took her arm, and led her into one of the small pantries beside the passage. He shut the door behind him, and heard, through the pine panels, de la Maine shouting at his people to get back to work.

"Lea?"

He turned. She stared up at him, her face white. She was wearing a high-neck dress, a soft blue color.

"He's dead, Sarah."

She gasped as if he'd hit her, and took a step back and shook her head. But she didn't say anything. She kept looking at him.

"My fault. I was just a little slow seeing them."

She didn't say a word.

"He . . . he and his men charged the Cossacks, and killed some of them. Abe was shot through the heart, riding into them."

"Oh . . . my . . . daddy," she said like a little girl. She swayed against Lea and pressed her face against his sheepskin coat, holding onto him as if she were going to fall.

She stayed that way for a little while and she didn't say anything more.

Sarah's face was still white as she sat in the library at her father's desk. She hadn't cried, and she wasn't crying now.

Lea and Leo Drexel were sitting in armchairs, facing her.

"My God, I'm sorry, Sarah. Abe was a dear friend to me," Drexel said. He tugged a fine lawn handkerchief from his sleeve and blew his nose.

"Thank you, Leo," she said. "Father died, I think, the way he would have wanted to." She glanced at Lea. "Now, the question is, what can *we* do?"

"The Count was killed, *and* all of his men?" Leo stared at Lea.

"Every damn one."

"Good God almighty." Leo dabbed at his forehead with the handkerchief. "That must have been a *battle* out there!"

"Yes, Mr. Drexel, it was."

"But then, haven't we won?" Sarah said.

"No," Lea said, "we haven't. The silver is out there. And Larrabee is still at Gunstock. We've cut off his right arm, but in a few days he'll grow another one."

194

"Shane, or Shannon, or whatever his name is."

"Yes, Mr. Drexel."

"And what if I tell Larrabee to get out of Gunstock tonight!" Sarah clenched her small fist and brought it down hard on the desk blotter.

"He'll go," Drexel said. "But—"

"But he'll leave some bought-and-paid-for people behind. And we don't know who they might be," Lea finished.

"Exactly," Drexel said.

"There's a simple way out of this, you know," Lea said. "I can kill the old man now. He has no one with him to stop me—not yet."

Drexel stared at him. "You're not serious?"

"As serious as taxes," Lea said.

"No . . . no, we can't do that," Sarah said, her eyes wide.

"It's the only way. I can kill him and be gone. With Larrabee dead, you'll have time to get to Boise, to make your own business arrangements about that silver. Contacts with companies that'll keep men like Larrabee from robbing you."

"No," Sarah said. "I couldn't. I couldn't do that!"

"It's impossible, Lea!" Drexel said. "Even if Sarah could countenance such a thing. You just don't understand this business! If a man like Larrabee were to be shot—murdered—at Gunstock, we'd be ruined! All the silver in the world wouldn't save us!"

"I couldn't do it anyway, Leo." She looked at Lea and tried to smile. "It . . . it is a generous thing to offer to sacrifice yourself that way, Lea. To turn yourself into a . . . a hunted killer."

"I'm sorry if I've upset you," Lea said and got up.

"We'll think of another way to handle Larrabee."

"Yes," she sighed, "we'll have to."

"Well, we have to decide something," Drexel said, standing up. "Among other things, we're going to miss Abe dreadfully when it comes to *managing* the hotel. We're going to need help with the suppliers for a start."

"Yes, I know," Sarah said. "I . . . I thought of sending a telegram to that young man that father liked at the Parker House. Father said he knew his business, said he was a first-class manager."

"At the Parker House? Oh, yes, you mean Henry Morganstern." He made a face. "That's all we need now, a Jew at Gunstock!"

"Father said he was very good."

"So I suppose he is," Drexel said, "if he'll come and work for less than an arm and a leg. If that insane old man hasn't had us all killed before he gets here!"

"If you will excuse me," Lea said, "I'll be getting out to my cabin. Edwards is supposed to see me out there when he finishes with Tiny." He walked to the door.

"Lea, wait!" Sarah called.

"Yes?"

"Lea, I didn't know you were hurt!"

"It's not serious."

"I . . . I would feel much better if you could stay up at the main building," she said. "They've already sent a man to kill you out in that cabin. Please stay up here at the hotel."

"Don't be a fool, man," Drexel said, as Lea hesitated. "We can't afford to lose you. It's that simple."

"All right."

"Good man." Drexel came to the door. "I'll see you settled. We'll put you into your old sick-room on the second floor. You'll feel right at home!"

Outside, in the corridor, Lea saw a short, broad-shouldered woman sitting by the door in a straight-back chair. It was the woman he'd seen with Sarah in the kitchen. She had a knitting bag on her lap. She stared at Lea and Drexel with cold brown eyes as they went by.

"Sarah's bodyguard?" Lea said as they walked down the hall.

"Oh, Mrs. Gomez. Yes, I believe she is. God knows she's savage enough. Went for de la Maine with a knife once, I believe. They had a disagreement about pastry dough."

"Listen, Drexel."

"Yes?"

"I meant what I said about Larrabee."

"Oh, I'm sure you did. As it happens, I agree with you entirely. But, really, Lea. I may call you Lea, I hope?"

"Yes."

"But really, I *don't* advise discussing cold-blooded murder in front of Sarah. She's a darling, and I love her dearly. As much, I think, as if she were my own daughter. She is a very nice and well-bred young lady. She has considerable difficulty in ordering the slaughter of lambs at Easter. Do I make my point?"

Lea laughed.

"I see I do." He led the way up a wide, carpeted staircase. "By the way, I'll have Edwards come straight to your room when he's finished with Morgan in the stables."

Drexel stopped on the stair landing and turned to face Lea. "How badly, may I ask, are you hurt? You seem

197

to move well enough."

"It hurts enough, but it's not serious."

"My God," Drexel said. "You men of action . . ." He turned to continue up the stairs.

"About Larrabee . . ."

Drexel turned, halfway up the staircase, and looked back down at Lea.

"I said, Lea, that I agreed with your *appreciation* of the situation. Larrabee is responsible for murdering one of the very few friends I have ever made in this world, and is, thereby, also responsible for hurting Sarah." He turned and continued up the stairs. "I take such things personally," he said.

Dr. Edwards came up to Lea's room a half hour later.

"You seem to be making a habit of being shot or stabbed in my bailiwick, Mr. Lea! I do wish you'd exercise a little prudence."

He stripped Lea's shift off, and examined both wounds—the old and the new. "Yes indeed—just a little prudence. I will say, though, that the shot wound might have been a good deal worse. Go and sit on the bed please."

Edwards cleaned the gunshot wound under Lea's arm, which hurt more than a little. Then he swabbed it with a disinfectant, and bandaged it lightly, wrapping the gauze ties around Lea's chest.

He took longer over the old knife wound, picking away the scabs along the puffed and inflamed stitches down Lea's side, swabbing each area as he finished.

"You have some bad bruising here, Lea. I believe you've torn some of the damaged tissue under the sutures. I've cleaned the wound, and the stitches have held, but you'd be well-advised to rest as much as you can for the next few days. You've got to give this a chance to heal, man!''

"Thank you, doctor."

Edwards stood up, closed his bag, and picked it up. "By the way," he said. "If only half of what I hear is accurate, you seem to have been instrumental in performing some rough justice on a number of a very unpleasant people." He cleared his throat. "You, that Indian of yours, and Tiny Morgan seem to be the heroes of the day." He walked to the door. Lea saw that Edwards had his knickers and climbing shoes on.

Edwards turned at the door. "Mr. Bridge," he said, "was a very fine man. A diamond in the rough men of that sort are called, I believe." He walked out and closed the door behind him.

Lea was getting his shirt back on when there was a knock on the door. He got up from the bed.

"Yes?"

"Room service, sir." It was Leo Drexel's voice.

"Come on in."

The door swung open, and a waiter pushed a dinner trolley into the room. Leo came in after him, and one of the bellmen came in after Leo, carrying Lea's bedroll, saddlebags.

"A good dinner—direct, I should add, from de la Maine's stove—and what is apparently the sum of your worldly goods." He signaled to the bellman to leave the bedroll and the rest beside the sofa. He nodded to Lea, and shooed the other men out of the room before him.

He paused at the door as Edwards had.

"Have a good night's sleep, Lea; you've earned it."

It was only late afternoon. Early for dinner, and early for bed. Edwards must have had a word with

Leo Drexel.

But Lea wasn't sorry. He felt tired to his bones. Tired of the riding and the killing and the fear. He had thought he was a dead man sure when the Count sat smiling, looking down at him with that nickel-plated pistol in his hand.

A year ago he had thought that at Gunstock he had found at last a place to rest easy. Lea laughed and went to take the covers off his dinner.

De la Maine had sent up a small steak, green beans from the kitchen gardens, hot rolls, butter, a wedge of apple pie, and a pitcher of milk. The Frenchman was a sensible man.

Lea pulled up a chair, and dug in. As he ate, he noticed his grimy hands, smudged with dirt, and speckled black from his pistol's exploding powder. After dinner, he'd get the chambermaids to bring up a tub, and hot water.

He slept a rich, dark, deep sleep. He woke once to hear a gust of wind hum down the chimney, the tick and hiss of the dying coals in the grate. Then he slept again.

Much later, hours later, he heard a key turning in the door lock.

Then he was awake, and sliding off the bed with the Colt in his hand. There was moonlight in the room. Shining softly in through the high windows. Not much light—but enough.

Lea watched the door as the lock clicked open. There was a pause. The door was closed, and then swung in again a way. Lea ran out of patience. He crossed the room quickly and quietly, stepped to the side, swung the door open, and brought up the Colt.

Sarah Bridge stood startled in the lamplit hall, staring at him, the revolver, and his naked body. Her pale face slowly flushed pink.

"Oh . . . oh, I—"

"You could have got yourself shot, you little fool!"

Lea reached out, took her arm, and pulled her into the room.

Then, he closed the door, felt for his key where it had fallen onto the carpet, and locked the door again. He picked up the chair and wedged it under the knob.

Sarah was standing in the moonlight by the windows.

"Lea . . . I'm sorry. It was terribly stupid of me."

"Where's that damned woman who's supposed to be watching you?"

"She . . . she's asleep."

"Very useful." He found his trousers across a chair by the bed and pulled them on.

Sarah Bridge stood in the moonlight, her face turned away from him as he buttoned the trousers.

"I'm sorry," she said. "I . . . I felt lonely."

Lea walked over to her. She was wearing a rich, long-sleeved dressing gown. The lace on it was white in the moonlight. Her eyes were shadowed dark. He couldn't see what she was thinking.

"You shouldn't be here," he said.

She shook her head. "I believe you're wrong. I believe I should be here."

"What do you want, Sarah? Do you want me to comfort you for the loss of your father?"

"Yes," she said, and put her hand up against his chest. "Yes, I do."

Lea put his arms around her and held her, then

tightened his arms to hold her closer. She felt small and slender in his arms. But he felt her breasts against him.

He held her for a while, and he felt his cock begin to rise against the softness of the dressing gown, against her soft belly.

It was time to let her go.

He took his arms from around her. "It's time you went back to your room," he said, and his voice was hoarse.

"No," she said, "Let me stay."

She stood in front of him with the moonlight dusting her hair. When he put up his hands and touched her, she was trembling.

CHAPTER TWENTY-THREE

Lea felt for the fasteners of her long dressing gown and found them. A row of little buttons down the front.

She stood still in the moonlight, her face in shadow. Lea carefully undid the buttons, one by one. He had to kneel before her to finish unfastening the last of them. Then he stood and tugged the gown from her shoulders. It fell around her with a soft rustle of silk, and lay in the moonlight at her feet.

She had only a gauzy nightgown on now. It shone in the light from the windows.

Lea put his hand on her slim throat, and felt her quick pulse against his palm. Her skin was warm and smooth as glass.

He bent and gathered up the hem of the nightgown and, as he lifted it, Sarah raised her arms over her head like an obedient child, so that he could slip it off. He lifted it slowly. And then he let it fall to the floor.

She stood naked in moonlight. Lea had never seen any single thing as beautiful as Sarah Bridge just then. Her legs were long and slender. Long, round thighs

flowed up into a sudden triangle of dark thick curls
and around into two high round buttocks, clenche
and tense.

Lea walked slowly around her as she stood, trem
bling. The faint and delicate muscles of her slim bac
made the slightest shadow along her spine. Some of he
dark hair, loosely coiled at the nape of her neck, ha
been disturbed when the nightgown was drawn off he
and dark, gleaming strands fell across her whit
shoulder, down her back.

When he stood in front of her again, Lea looke
down at her shadowed face. Her naked breasts shook
little with her breathing. For such a slight girl, she ha
large breasts, shaped like rounded pears. They wer
shadowed. Lea reached to grip her slim shoulders an
gently turned her toward the light. Her breast
trembled as he turned her, and the moonlight shone o
them. The nipples were swollen.

Lea took his hands from her shoulders and put ther
on her breasts. He lifted them in his hands, weighin
them, squeezing them with his long fingers. He too
the nipples and pinched them.

She gasped.

"Am I hurting you?"

She looked up at him. He could see her eyes in th
moonlight, dark, clear blue.

He gathered her breasts in his hands, and squeeze
them.

"Am I hurting you?"

"No," she said. Her voice was hoarse. "You're no
hurting me."

He reached down and put his hand between her leg
She tried to back away from him, but he squeezed he

breast with his other hand and wouldn't let her go.

He felt the thick hair between her legs, and found a small slippery place. He held her still and stroked the place with his finger. She stood quiet and let him do it.

Still stroking her there, he took his hand from her breast and bent to take the nipple in his mouth. He sucked on it, and bit into her gently.

"Ohh-oh!" She twisted against him, pushing against him as he mouthed her breast. His finger, between her legs, found a small wet place, warmer, wetter than the rest. He twisted his finger and opened the wet place up. He drew his finger along a little slit. It was slippery.

He took his mouth off her breast and looked down, and saw that she was standing up on her toes, straining up to him. His finger was hooked inside her. Her nipple was wet from his mouth.

"Please," she said.

"Please what?"

"I don't know."

He moved his finger deeper into her, and saw that she was on her toes again, straining as he pushed the finger in. He felt something against the tip, touched it, and pushed again.

"Oh, you hurt me!"

Lea pulled his finger out of her and stepped back. She was standing alone, sweating. Her mouth was open a little. He could hear her breathing as she swayed toward him.

Lea reached down and unbuttoned his trousers. She watched him as he let them fall.

She looked down at him.

Lea stepped to her, bent, and picked her up in his arms.

He cradled her for a moment, feeling the slight, smooth, naked length of her lying across his arms, against his chest. Her head was back, her dark hair falling free. A delicate perfume rose from her—a mingled scent of violets, the sweet smell of a young girl's skin.

He carried her to the bed.

She lay still across it, half in shadow. Lea could see her eyes, her white face, shining in the darkness.

"Here," he said. He took her hand and put it on his cock. He felt her tremble. Slowly, she curled her fingers around it, held it, still staring up at him.

"That's what you need, isn't it?" he said.

"Yes, I need you," she said softly, her voice shaking.

He bent down and kissed her. He kissed Sarah Bridge as he hadn't kissed a woman in many years. He gave to her as much as he took. He felt her hand release him, and her long, slim arms came up around him and held him to her. He felt her breasts crushing against his chest. She kissed and sucked at his mouth as if she were starving.

He pulled away from her, slid down and put his hands under the backs of her knees, then lifted her long, bare legs up, spreading them wide. He smelled the faint odor of her sex.

He took his cock in his hand, pressed the swollen tip into the damp curls at her crotch, and began to thrust himself into her.

Sarah gasped, and started to struggle against him, but he reached up and took her wrists and held them down against the pillows. He found her mouth with his, and kissed her and bit at her lips, gently, until she lay still under him, panting, her breath hot in his mouth.

He felt the warm, wet, close grip of her around the head of his cock wet curls against him. Her heart was pounding; he felt it against his chest. Lea drove into her.

Sarah screamed into his mouth, twisting frantically under him. He was locked deep into her, in a wet squeezing heat that made him shake with pleasure.

She tore her mouth away from his. "Oh, please . . . don't! You're hurting—"

He pulled out of her, only a little way, and she gasped again. He let go of her wrists and reached down to grip her soft buttocks with his hands. Gathering the cool, round flesh in his fingers, he held it tightly.

He pulled his cock out of her a little farther, and felt the coolness as the air touched him.

He lifted her buttocks and drove into her again. His cock made a wet sound as it plunged into her. And the girl cried out and her long thighs thrashed against his sides. The quiet room was filled with the wet, smacking noises.

Suddenly Sarah reached up to hold him, her nails digging into his shoulders as he moved above her.

"Oh . . . *oh!*" Her slender body, drenched with sweat, twisted and bucked beneath him. "Oh, God!"

Her long, pale, slim legs thrashed, and wrapped themselves around him. Her round buttocks were bunched in his hands as he lifted her to him, driving his cock deep into her, grinding against the soft, wet cushion of her mound.

Lea felt a flood of pleasure rising from his balls, from the small of his back, an ache of pleasure so sweet that it hurt him.

Lea began to move faster in her, gasping in the agony of pleasure, driving into her harder and faster.

"Oh, please—" She clawed at his back, her white face contorted in the shadows. "Oh . . . oh, *please!* Crying, calling like a cat, she came.

And Lea came with her. He groaned and trembled and pumped into her until he thought it would kill him.

He still moved on her, and she moved with him. Both slippery, moving slowly, holding each other, bending his head to her, lifting her face to kiss.

"I'm so . . . glad," she whispered.

Lea lay with his full weight upon her, sliding against her with their sweat and juices. She grunted like a puppy with the pleasure of it, and reach up again to hug him.

"Sarah . . . I love you," Lea said. And was surprised to hear himself say it. It had been weary years since he'd said that—and there'd been only two girls he'd ever said it to.

One was dead—dead by his hand as sure as if he'd shot her down himself. The other was living—and happy, he hoped—a long way from Gunstock.

This girl was too young for him. Too rich, too brave and too beautiful.

When he tried to get up, Sarah hugged him to her and wouldn't let him go. So he closed his eyes, there in the shadowed moonlight, and held her, stroking her sweat-damp hair, and pretended she was his forever.

In the morning she was gone. Gone, and left him sleeping like a boy.

He woke to the sun streaming in through the tall windows and stretched, grunting at the twinge along his side. (Dr. Edwards would have said it served him right.)

He lay there for a few moments, remembering, then yawned and stretched again, a long, luxurious stretch. To hell with the side *and* Dr. Edwards!

He had to piss. And he needed a hell of a breakfast, the best and biggest breakfast the Frenchman could make!

He threw the sheets aside, then bent to sniff at them. They smelled of sex. There were four small spots of blood on the bottom sheet. Where I hurt her, Lea thought, being such a fine stud of a fellow. He covered the place and got out of bed.

Outside, in the corridor, Lea found a straight-back chair against the wall beside the door. There was a strand of gray wool yarn on the carpet. Garciela Gomez had kept her watch after all.

Going down the east stairway, Lea passed a group of guests coming up from breakfast. They were English people, a family named Sutherland. "Good morning to you, Lea!" He'd shot mule deer with Sutherland when they'd first come. "Morning, Mr. Sutherland."

The lady and the children nodded and went on their way. "I say, Lea, what chance do you think of a bear before it snows? One of your big browns, or cinnamons?" Lea leaned against the bannister and thought a moment. "Those are shy bears, Mr. Sutherland. Might be better to go packing down to the Salmon, try for a grizzly this time of year."

The Englishman's cheeks flushed over his ginger whiskers. "Ah, so I said, so I said! But Florence won't hear of it. She's got some notion into her head about that French banker fellow that was eaten by the grizzlies! She won't hear of it! Says I may shoot anything I please, says I may shoot a blasted *camel* if I wish! But I am not to hunt one of those grizzly bears! What do you think of that?''

Lea laughed. "Well, they can be dangerous. But men with heavy rifles usually knock them over without too much trouble." He considered the problem for a moment. "Tell you what. If you should want a *real* trophy—a *hunter's* trophy—you might try High Pass for bighorn sheep. There's a ram up there with horns as big as a house. Some men have tried for him, but they haven't gotten him. It's very rough up there, you see. Damn high, and damn cold. It's hard going.''

Sutherland lit up like theater limelight. "I say! You do think I might get a shot at it? if I can stand the gaff?''

"I think so. Ask Davies to take you up past Ship Rock. He'll know the place. But remember to stick close to him up there; it'll be damn cold.''

"Damned if I don't do it!" Sutherland said. "But aren't you going to be guiding?''

"Not this week, Mr. Sutherland. I have to stay at the hotel the next few days. Expecting someone.''

"Oh, bad luck!''

"No. Good luck to you with that ram. Davies is a very good man.''

Sutherland shook Lea's hand. "Thanks for the tip, old man, though I do wish we could go up together.''

"Perhaps another time," Lea said. "And remember, people shooting uphill tend to hold too low.''

The Englishman smiled. "Right." And went bounding up the stairs. So, not all the guests at Gunstock knew about Abe's death, and the fight with the Cossacks. Sarah and Drexel have their work cut out keeping it even half quiet.

Lea went down the stairs to the lobby. He was

210

wondering if he'd see Sarah there, or perhaps in the kitchen, talking to de le Maine.

He met Larrabee in the lobby.

The old man came strolling across the gleaming marble flooring as Lea reached the foot of the staircase.

Larrabee was dressed like an Eastern college football player—dark, baggy, knickers, canvas shoes, and a blue, turtleneck sweater. His small paunch bulged against the wool.

"Amazing!" he said, coming up to Lea with a merry smile. "Really extraordinary! what a fellow you must be, Mr. Lea!" He stretched out a small pink hand, and took Lea's hand and shook it. "To defeat *that* man—and his *men*—in a fight is no small matter!" He gave Lea's hand another shake before letting it go. The old man couldn't have seemed more pleased at the way things had gone at Fork Creek. He also didn't seem to give a damn who heard about it now.

He was a very clever old man. Lea knew what he was doing, and admired him for it. Larrabee was telling Lea that he had no chance at all. That even the most spectacular victory was no real victory. It was in fact, only an interesting, temporary variation in a losing game.

"It will be most interesting to see how you and Shannon hit it off," the old man said, and smiled, eyes bright. He winked and went on his way.

CHAPTER TWENTY-FOUR

Jonathan Pierce Larrabee wasn't really as pleased as all
that.

He was mighty angry, if truth be told. Not with the
deceased Count Orloff and his blundering Cossacks. He
was angry at himself.

The old man, hands tucked into his knicker pockets,
was strolling downstairs to the hotel gymnasium for his
routine massage and steam. He considered his errors as
he went.

*Am I becoming an old fool? To send that posturing
medieval ass and his serfs to fight Abe Bridge and his
men in their own mountains? To say nothing of Lea.
What an odd hunting guide that fellow makes. If it
weren't for Shane's coming, it might be interesting to
have the Pinkertons look into our Mr. Lea. However,
Shannon will likely make such an inquiry moot.*

*Difficult . . . difficult. Bridge dead, the girl alive and
surrounded by friends . . . hotel guests. Not the sort of
people you can murder a girl in front of. A little too
important for that. A little too well connected for that.*

Can't bring in a parcel of bully boys and simply take the damn place over, not with a stack of English lords and Boston Brahmins looking on. Too damned raw!

Larrabee pushed his way through the green baize door at the foot of the stairs and, smiling pleasantly, greeted the Indian boy who worked as attendant. Drexel's Nancy-boy if his information was correct. Might be something to see how the sissy stood up to a little pressure. Get Drexel, and *he* might well be able to handle the girl.

He walked into the dressing room, nodded to George Chapin, the only other man there, and began undressing. *There's one of the Boston jackasses, right there*, he thought. *Couldn't hold onto sixty miles of track, himself, so he went whining to that Jew, Brandeis.*

Chapin put on his jacket, wished Larrabee a cold good day, and walked out.

Good riddance, you fart.

Larrabee wrapped a towel around his plump, pink middle, and went to get his massage.

The boy had good hands, though God only knows where they'd been. Larrabee lay grunting softly as the young Peigan massaged the muscles along his spine, worked the stiffness from his neck. A good massage; relaxed a man, gave him time to think, put him in a good frame of mind.

The boy worked lower, at the small of the back, pressing, stroking, easing out the knots. And what to do about Morgan? A nice question. It was considerably more important than the brawls out here in Idaho, though perhaps not more important than a mountain full of silver. Morgan couldn't be fought, and he couldn't be fooled. That was the long and short of it.

Larrabee sighed and turned over on his back. The young Indian began to massage his chest, rubbing in easy, circular motions. J.P. Morgan's time might yet come, but it would take the government to bring him down. There was a notion! What the devil was he paying a senator *for,* if not for service to be rendered.

Better not to rush, though. Still, it was something to think about. In the meantime he'd give Morgan the debentures. It was hard to let them go, and stupid to try and keep them from him.

The Peigan had worked down his legs, and was massaging his feet, working his thumbs gently into the instep. A brisk rub at the soles of the feet was better than a foot bath any day. That doctor was a fool.

The boy finished, and stood back from the table. Larrabee grunted and sat up, tying his towel around his waist.

"Good rubdown, boy!"

The Indian didn't even smile. He just stood there, dumb as a post, as would a cigar-store Indian.

The Peigan ushered him into the steamroom, empty this early in the day, seated Larrabee in the first cabinet, closed the heavy maple double-doors, and brought another towel to wrap around his neck, to keep the rising steam out of his face.

"Only a few minutes today."

The Indian boy nodded, expressionless, and went to the wall to open the steam valve a quarter turn.

Larrabee heard the hiss and felt the warm breath against his legs.

The Peigan went to the corner of the room, picked up the mop there, and brought it back to the steam cabinet. While Larrabee watched, puzzled, he quickly pushed the mop handle through the brass grips on the cabinet doors.

"What the hell is that? What are you doing?"

Larrabee kicked hard against the heavy cabinet doors, and hurt his foot.

"You God-damned jackass! Get that damn thing out of the door!"

The Indian boy went to the steam valve and opened it a full turn.

Larrabee sat goggling at him, staring in shock, and felt what seemed for a moment to be a flood of ice-cold water rush in against his legs. It seemed for only a moment. Then the live steam began to cook his legs.

Larrabee yelled in pain and tried to stand, to struggle free of the heavy cabinet, slamming into it with his shoulders, kicking wildly at the solid doors. He screamed and heaved up and down, billows of scalding steam escaping, rolling up out of the neck of the cabinet, burning his face as he howled and kicked.

The Indian boy was gone. He was out of the steamroom, into the cool, small paneled gymnasium, and out through the green baize door. The Peigan locked it behind him, and leaned a neatly lettered sign against it. CLOSED FOR LUNCH—WILL BE OPEN AT 2 O'CLOCK. Then, he went upstairs. It was time for Mr. Drexel's lunch.

In the steamroom, Larrabee no longer screamed, or struggled. He sat still—in a hissing, roaring cloud of steam. His face was a very dark red, and his eyes and his mouth were open.

"Oh! How *could* you? How could you do such a thing!" Sarah's eyes were filled with angry tears.

215

The three of them were in the library again, and Lea was sighing at the memory of a golden breakfast—a late breakfast—in the servant's dining room. He and Sarah had eaten quietly there together, with no one else to bother them. Bacon and blueberry muffins—and kissing. That's what the breakfast had been. And now this.

Sarah sat at the desk, her face buried in her hands.

"To . . . to *murder* a man. Here! My father never would have wanted it. He never would have wanted *that!*"

Lea had his own opinion on that score, but he felt that the better part of valor, in this case, was to keep his big mouth shut. But it hurt to see Sarah so damn upset by it.

Drexel was the one who got up and went to her. He leaned over the desk and put his hand on her shoulder. She looked up as she angrily shrugged the hand away, and blushed to see that it was Drexel, not Lea.

"I'm sorry, Leo. What Lea has done is my fault."

"But *Lea* hasn't done anything, my dear."

"What?"

Drexel turned to give Lea a sardonic glance.

"Though apparently he's too much the gentleman to defend himself against a lady's accusations."

Lea didn't say a word. He just sat back in the leather-covered easy chair and took it all in.

"You see, dear, Lea didn't know a thing about this tragic affair, and didn't have a damn thing to do with it. I assure you, it's all been news to him!"

Sarah sniffed and searched for her handkerchief. She didn't look at Lea. "Then . . . then why—" She found her handkerchief, and blew her nose. "Then how did it *happen?*"

"It was my fault, I think." Drexel sighed. "I believe I spoke a little too plainly once in Hunting-moon's presence."

"Then he—"

"Yes, I'm afraid the poor boy assumed that I'd be *pleased,* that I'd be overjoyed at his barbaric demonstration of loyalty."

Leo sighed again. "The boy *is* a savage, after all."

"Dreadful," Lea said.

"Oh, yes," said Sarah. "But . . . but what can we *do?*"

"Well," Drexel said, "you may blame me for this, but I took it upon myself to send the boy away. Back to his own people. It didn't seem fair that he should be judged by *our* laws, particularly since it was I, after all, who probably put the idea into his head!"

"Nobly put," said Lea.

"Yes," Sarah said. She looked at Lea and blushed. "Yes, I think that you were right to do that. Mr. Larrabee *was* responsible for my father's death."

Drexel looked thoughtful. "I suppose," he said, "that it *is* a sort of rough justice."

"Yes," she said, "I think it is."

"No question," said Lea.

She glanced at Lea and blushed again. "I owe you an apology, Lea, I—"

"You owe me nothing, Miss Bridge."

"Oh, I think you can call her Sarah," Drexel said, with a sardonic look.

"You owe me nothing. I *would* have killed the old man if you'd let me."

"Well, well—that's all very nice, but not to the point," Drexel said. "Let us remember that we do still have Mr. Larrabee on our hands."

"We'll have to say it was an accident."

"My dear Sarah, an accident of that kind could ruin Gunstock as completely as a murder might have! No, no. It won't do. However, I have had a notion."

"I don't doubt it," Lea said.

"I have had a notion. Mr. Larrabee was a very elderly man. And a man, moreover, without any immediate family—certainly no one who cared very much for him."

"But Leo—"

"No, dear, let me finish. So, I took it upon myself to inform certain guests that Mr. Larrabee had had a stroke while in the steam room. And, unfortunately, it had proved fatal."

"Considering Larrabee's condition, Leo, it's going to be a little difficult to make that bird fly, isn't it?" said Lea.

"Not at all," said Leo. "Not at all. I have consulted with our mountain-climbing physician, and have extracted from him a professional diagnosis *and* death certificate indicating a severe stroke."

"Oh, heavens."

"Now dear, don't concern yourself with these details. Leave them to me."

"And when the body goes back east?" Lea said.

Leo pursed his lips. "Well, I have telegraphed Larrabee's nephew in New York, informed him of the tragedy, and, since I had understood it to be his uncle's fondest wish, suggested that Mr. Larrabee might remain right here, at Gunstock, in the mountains he so dearly loved."

218

"Touching," said Lea.

"Oh, goodness."

"Goodness, dear Sarah," said Leo, "has nothing to do with it." He walked to the door. "And I'm off to make certain that our earnest young physician doesn't backslide."

"Just a minute," Lea said, and got up to go out with him. "I'll be back in a moment, Sarah."

When the library door was closed behind them, Lea said, quietly, "Well done, Mr. Drexel."

Drexel gave him a weary smile. "Yes, I think it *was* done fairly well."

"And the Indian boy?"

"Oh, I gave him enough money to buy a great many ponies, and sent him on his way. Frankly, until this matter came up, I think he considered me something of a bore."

"And the doctor?"

"The doctor, it seems, has become fond of us. Or fond of Gunstock, which amounts to the same thing. And now, Mr. Lea, having done my part in our little drama, I must inform you that, alas, your turn has come again, and perhaps, I'm sorry to say, with an added complication."

"Which is?"

"Tomorrow, a rather minor literary figure is to arrive at Gunstock for a short stay. His name is Ned Buntline, famous among *afficianados* of penny-dreadful tales of famous Western outlaws, killers, and so on. I understand he's met most of that crowd and is very familiar with them."

"And you thought his arrival might be important

to me?''

"Isn't it?''

Lea thought for a moment, then he said: "Yes, it might be damned important.''

"So I was afraid. There's worse news yet.''

"What?''

"A man named Shannon came into Salmon on the mail-coach yesterday afternoon.''

"He'll be here tomorrow night.''

"I believe he will.''

"All right." Lea turned to go back into the library. "Thank you, Drexel.''

"You don't have to thank me, Lea. Anyone who injured my friends—or Gunstock—would find me ready to do them any harm I could." He nodded, turned and walked off down the corridor.

Lea went back into the library. Sarah was in his arms before he could close the door behind him.

"Forgive me! Do you forgive me?''

"There's nothing to forgive, sweetheart," he said, and bent his head to kiss her hair.

"And now there'll be no trouble," she said. "Larrabee's dead. That gunman won't come. You can stay here forever.''

Lea lifted her small chin with his finger, and kissed her.

"The gunman *is* coming. He'll be here tomorrow. Leo just told me.''

Her face grew pale. "But he won't do anything! He'll find out that Larrabee's dead—and then there's no *reason!*''

"Unless he's already been paid to do his job.''

"But even so, Larrabee's *dead!* Who would *care* whether he . . . he did his job?"

"He might care," Lea said.

CHAPTER TWENTY-FIVE

That night, she came to Lea's room again.

They had their dinner brought up, and they sat beside the fire, eating and drinking the pink champagne that de la Maine had sent up to them. They listened to the northern wind sighing through the ramparts of Gunstock.

"Lea," Sarah said to him, "am I an awful girl, to be here with you, to do the things we do, with Daddy just murdered and buried in those mountains?"

Lea reached across the table, and gently stroked her cheek. "Are you happy, Sarah?" he said.

She smiled. "Yes," she said. "I'm the happiest, I think, I've ever been."

"Then Abe would be happy for you."

"Yes," she said. "Yes, I *think* he would be." She laughed. "But he'd be happier if I was married." She blushed furiously and covered her face with her hands. "Oh, no! I'm . . . I'm *sorry!* I didn't have any *idea* I was going to say that!"

Lea sat back in his chair and laughed. "You trying to

frighten me away?''

''No.'' She put her hands down, and sat up in her chair, her face still red.

''Sarah,'' Lea said, ''I'll never be able to marry you.'' She had to be told, and the sooner, the better.

''I see,'' she said, and bit her lip, but didn't say anything more.

''No, you don't see,'' Lea said. ''It has nothing to do with you.''

''Nothing to do—''

''No. It has to do with me.''

''I don't— Are you . . . married?''

''No.''

''But then—''

''Sarah, my name's not Farris Lea.''

''I don't care! I don't care. A lot of men have changed their names out here. I don't care what you did!''

''My name—''

''I don't care!'' she interrupted him. Please—''

''I'm Frank Leslie,'' he said. ''Sometimes people called me Buckskin Frank Leslie.''

Sarah sat staring at him. ''But . . . but you're *famous.*''

Lea smiled grimly. ''That's one word for it.''

''You . . . you were with Wyatt Earp and Doc Holliday. . . and . . . and all *those* people.''

''Yes.''

She was clenching her hands together on the white tablecloth before her. The knuckles were white with tension.

She tried to smile. ''Did you rob banks or something? I wouldn't care!''

''No, I didn't rob banks. I . . . I killed people, Sarah.

223

For a living.''

Sarah said nothing.

"I've killed about forty people now." It was a dreadful relief to say it, to tell it to her. "Most of them were fair fights, I think. If it *can* be fair when I gunfight with a man."

"Well," Sarah said, "you fought here, and you killed men here. Thank God you did!" She lifted her glass of champagne with a a trembling hand, and drank from it. "So, if that's all—"

"It isn't all, Sarah. I was a professional gambler, too. And a pimp—a *mack*. You know what that is?"

"Yes," she said, and blushed. "I know what that is. It's—it's being a . . . a bodyguard in a disorderly house!"

"No. It's living off the girls there. And it's going out and bringing girls into the life. And it's beating them when they want to leave."

Sarah sat looking at him, trying to smile, but she was crying. "You never did that!" she said.

"I did it for years. And I took money to frighten men, and sometimes to force those frightened men to fight me so I could shoot them to death."

"No." She shook her head. "No, you didn't."

Lea reached across the table and took her hands in his. "Dear heart," he said, "for all those years, I was as vicious a dog as any man *could* be—and I enjoyed it."

"All right, then!" She pulled her hands away. "Then why did you come here? Why are you the way you are now?"

"It happened that I loved a girl. Loved her as much as I love you, Sarah. I forced a fight on a man, just for the fun of it, and she was killed."

224

Lea got up from the table and walked to the windows. He looked out through the glass, past the bright reflections of the candles, out to the distant pines, their dark branches bending and swaying to the night wind.

"And that," he said, "finished that life for me, forever."

"Then," Sarah said from the table, "you . . . you can start a *new* life. Here at Gunstock!"

Lea came back to the table.

"Sarah, have you heard of Wes Hardin? Ben Thompson? Clay Allison? Have you heard of a man named Frank Pace?"

"Yes," she said, "I've heard of those men."

Lea stood, looking down at her. "There is not one of those men—not one—who, if he heard I was alive, and knew where to find me, wouldn't come looking to kill me." He sat back down at the table, and poured himself more champagne.

"They wouldn't find you, here. No one will know *who* you are!"

Lea smiled. "A writer named Buntline is checking into Gunstock tomorrow. He knows my face as well as I know yours. At least he did when I wore a beard and mustache. He's likely to recognize me anyway."

"All right!" She sat up straight. "Then we'll keep you hidden till he goes!"

"With Larrabee's gunman coming tomorrow as well?" He shook his head. "I've been lucky for the past year. After all, this hotel's not much of a likely spot for frontier riff-raff like me. It's only a question of time. Someone *will* recognize me, someday. And I'll have to run."

"But people love you here! We'll *protect* you!" She took her handkerchief from her reticule and blew her nose.

"And make a shooting-gallery out of your home? Out of Gunstock? No."

"If you loved me—"

He reached across the table and put his finger gently against her lips.

"*Because* I love you."

The next morning, Lea went out to the stables. He intended to stay out of the main building until Buntline had gone on his way. Damn the man for coming out to Gunstock. If Drexel weren't careful, Buntline would have the whole story out of the hotel help, and into the Eastern newspapers! Buntline was no fool.

Lea had met the writer in Hays, the year that Hickok was marshal. Buntline had been in his element then, sitting on the cool, shady, whorehouse porches, listening to buffalo-chips being thrown by every hoodlum and high-roller passing through. Listening, and writing it down as gospel. The secret of Buntline's great success with those nonsensical books of his, Lea thought, was that the man persuaded himself to believe the stuff. And so did his readers.

It made Hickok. Before Buntline, Bill had just been a well-known sport, fancy-man, and hoodlum for hire. He'd been very good with guns, of course. Bill'd always been good with guns. Those little books made Hickok —and killed him.

Lea'd seen Hickok years later, a few months before he went out to the Dakotas to get shot. He'd been a different man. Not so handsome anymore. He'd worn

226

spectacles to order his lunch.

In just a few years, his own name had eaten him up, the way the Indians say the coyote spirit eats a man up.

Lea stayed in the stables all morning, talking to Tiny and the other men coming by. Tiny talked to him for an hour about rainbows before Lea even remembered saying what he had that started it. Tiny was dead certain that Lea'd been right. No gold at the end of any rainbow anymore.

"That's for sure," Lea'd said. "I was damn sure right on that!"

"Yes," Tiny said.

"No question," said Lea, and asked how the Russian horses were thriving, mainly to get off the subject of rainbows. "Oh, *pretty* horses!" Tiny said. They all had come to like him and know he owned them for his own. Even the big black gelding!

Lea walked back with Tiny to the gelding's stall, and nearly got an ear bitten off for his pains. The black was quick, and had snaked his sleek head out over the stall door and taken his bite. Lea'd ducked just fast enough for those big yellow teeth to meet air instead of ear.

"That son-of-a-bitch is a killer!"

"No such-a-thing," Tiny replied. "We scared him, coming along the stalls that way. Should have sung-out!" He had more to say about how the Russian needed some plain old kindness and care. It was intended to be a grass-eating horse, not meant for grain.

Lea agreed with it all, and made sure to walk to the front of the stables by the tackroom instead of back by the Russian's stall. He said so-long to Tiny, walked out of the stable, and paused to light up the stub of a cigar.

Right then, as sure as fate, Ned Buntline and two

other men came walking straight toward him.

Lea kept his head bent over his cigar as he lit up, and the men came right up to him.

"Say there, Bud," Buntline said to him, "you have some riding horses in there for guests?"

"Yep," Lea said, gestured with the cigar to the stable doors, and added, "Right in there." He tried for a Southern accent as he said it, and then turned and strolled away, puffing on the cigar, and taking his time.

Ned had put on considerable flesh. And what were the odds he'd recognized Lea? Slim odds, Lea thought. No beard now, no mustache—and a lot of years gone by.

Now he'd have to go hide in the laundry!

That evening, he and Sarah were in his room. She hadn't talked more about marriage, or about what he'd said the night before. She sat, seeming contented enough, in a rocking chair she'd had the maid bring in. She sat by the fire, knitting away like a Granny at what looked to be the beginnings of a wool muffler in red and green stripes.

He should get up and go to her, and say, "My sweet love, I won't be here to wear it."

Someone knocked on the door. Lea supposed that it was dinner, but he picked his Colt off the table before he went to answer it.

It wasn't dinner. It was Leo Drexel, looking pale.

"What is it, Leo?"

"Leo? Come in!" Sarah called.

"No, dear—have to run! *He's here.*"

Lea stepped out into the corridor and closed the door behind him.

"Where is he?"

228

"Down in the lobby," Drexel said. "I told him to get out." He grimaced. "He declined. But he'd asked for Larrabee. He was surprised to hear he was dead."

"What did you think of him?"

"My dear fellow, that is your line of work, not mine! I'd say, however, that he was . . . a serious man."

Lea smiled, "I'll bet he is." He thought for a moment. "You go on about your business, Leo. Leave him to me."

"With pleasure."

"I'll go down and see what he's got in his mind to do."

Drexel held out his hand. "Good luck."

Lea smiled, and shook his hand. "It's only a matter of business, Leo."

"Yours, thank God," Drexel said, and turned and walked off down the corridor.

The door opened behind Lea, and Sarah put her head out. She looked very pale. "Is that man here?"

"You were listening, weren't you?" Lea said, and bent down to kiss her nose. "I'll go down and see what he's up to." He walked into the room, picked up his gunbelt, dropped the Colt into the holster, and strapped the belt on. Then he went to the bedside table, took the Arkansas toothpick out of the drawer, and slipped the blade down into his boot. He went to Sarah, took her in his arms, and hugged her. "Don't worry," he said. "I think it'll be talking, not shooting, tonight. What's for dinner?"

"You're not thinking of—"

"Inviting him? No, sweet, I'm just hungry."

She forced herself to laugh. "You're a dreadful man! We're having ham and greens, hot biscuits, and a fruit compote."

"Wonderful—real country. I'll be back up in a few minutes." And he was out the door. He knew he would be longer than a few minutes.

The Gunstock lobby was the size of a good-sized railroad station, but considerably more luxurious. It was crowded. The guests, most of them, enjoyed an evening stroll along the gleaming marble floors, the two-story pillars, the huge, nodding potted palms and rubber trees. It was an opportunity for the ladies to display their fine dresses from the house of Worth, in Paris and other finery.

Lea came down the main staircase and saw the gunman standing by a pillar near the entrance to the terrace.

He stood out from the rest like a cougar in a flock of penguins and peacocks.

He was wearing a long, fringed buckskin shirt, canvas trousers, and brown boots. He had a gunbelt around his waist.

Lea walked to the bottom of the stairs, nodded to Toby Easterby, who was squiring some handsome lady Lea didn't know, and went on across the lobby toward the terrace entrance.

Now he could see how the man wore his gun. High. High on the right side. Looked like a Peacemaker.

The man had seen him coming. He was watching him as he crossed the lobby.

Some people had stopped to look at them now. Nobody at Gunstock made much of a habit of strolling the lobby wearing guns.

Lea saw that the man had put his coat and hat down

on a chair beside a pillar. The coat was a beat-up sheepskin. Jobs must be few and far between.

Lea stepped around a group of guests talking about horse-racing at Saratoga. He walked up to the man.

"Shannon?"

"Yes," the man said.

He was a small man. Handsome, in a quiet way, with long, dark-blond hair, and blue eyes. Now that Lea was close, he could see some gray in the man's hair, some lines in his face.

"I think we have something to talk about, Shannon."

"I don't think so," the man said. He had a touch of the South to his speech.

Lea stood easy. They were just a few feet apart. The small man looked tired from traveling.

"Well," Lea said, "your man is gone. His try has gone with him. Any friends he has to follow up will be too little—and too late."

Shannon smiled a little; he seemed a decent sort of a man. "That's high-finance you're talking about Mr.—"

"Lea."

Shannon nodded. "I don't trouble myself with high finance, Mr. Lea."

"You've been paid?"

"Indeed I have." He'd stopped smiling.

"And you intend to earn that money?"

"Indeed I do."

"Cigar?" Lea dug into his jacket pocket for a cigar stub.

"No."

Lea lit his cigar, not troubling that both hands would be busy. He saw Shannon notice it, and got another grudging smile out of him.

"It seems a shame for us to be blowing holes in each other over a dead dog who wasn't worth much alive."

Shannon said nothing. Lea realized there'd be no waiting until morning with this one. No chance at all.

"Would you care to join me, and a young lady, for supper?"

Shannon laughed at Lea as if they were old friends, and shook his head. "Is she a fine looker?" he said.

"That, and a darling to boot."

"Then I'd better not," Shannon said. "She'd make me feel like a brute."

Here's a man I could like, Lea thought. *I can't turn him aside.*

The first bell rang for dinner and, throughout the huge lobby, the guests and their ladies began to drift toward the dining rooms.

"Would you care to step outside?" Lea said.

"No."

Thinks I might have people out there. Good man. I do like a careful man.

"Well now," Lea said. "That was a warning bell for dinner. They ring another one, a reminder, in about a minute, and most of these people will be out of here."

The small man nodded.

Lea walked over a few steps, to stub out his cigar in the dirt of a potted palm.

"You won't change your mind about this?" he said.

Shannon shook his head.

"Dammit, man, you likely have no chance against me!" Lea said.

The small man looked at him, then moved his head to one side, to see past Lea. Lea knew he was making certain the lobby was clear—no more people in the line

232

of fire.

The people were moving past them, talking, laughing. One or two men glanced back, looking at the two men with guns.

"Listen to me," Lea said. He supposed the man would think he was begging. "This is a fool's play! Take that old thief's money and ride! I say you'd have no chance against me, and I mean it."

Shannon said nothing. He stepped back a few paces, almost to the lobby wall. He was really quite a small man.

"Listen, dammit—my name's not Farris Lea!"

Shannon smiled at him. "I never thought it was," he said.

The second bell rang, and he drew. He was very fast.

Lea drew and shot him through the chest.

He found himself kneeling down on the cold marble. The cold green-veined marble gleamed in the lamplight. He thought he was in the gardens for a moment, kneeling on grass and roses.

"Oh, my God! *Oh, my God!*" Some woman was screaming.

His face felt like a piece of wood. A man was running to him. He heaved himself up and raised the Colt. He saw black dress shoes, not brown boots.

Toby Easterby was kneeling by him.

"Jesus Christ, man!" Toby held him by the arm. There was blood all over. The woman was still screaming.

"Get me up," he tried to say to Toby. But he didn't say anything. He couldn't feel his mouth. He put his left hand down into the blood and pushed himself up, got his feet under him.

Toby was still holding onto his arm. He pushed him away and looked for Shannon.

He swayed on his feet. If he looked too fast at something, he saw double. People were standing just a little way away, staring at him, staring at the gun in his hand.

He started to walk, just a few steps, to get out of the blood. It was on his boots. He looked over by the wall, and saw the small man there. Shannon was down.

Lea walked over there. It took some doing; his face was hurtng him terribly. He felt himself getting sick to his stomach. He took deep breaths to keep from vomiting in front of all these people.

Shannon was down, lying sprawled along the marble at the base of the wall. When Lea bent his head to look at him, he saw double. So he knelt down instead.

Shane was dead. Lea could see the blotch in the middle of the buckskin shirt where the round had hit him. His face didn't look as bad as most dead men's.

Toby was standing behind Lea, talking.

"Jesus!" he said. "Jesus, he was quick!"

Toby was a good boy. Didn't mind a little blood.

"Yes," Lea said. Now he could talk. But his voice sounded strange to him. Thick, muttering, like an animal's.

"Yes," Lea said, "that's Shannon. And he was fast on the draw."

"Let's get you up," said Toby Easterby. He took Lea by the arm again. Another man came to help him. They got Lea up. Toby took the Colt from him and put it in it's holster.

They walked him toward the grand staircase, but he shook them loose and walked on his own. He could hear the people talking, staring at him. One of the women was crying.

He could feel blood running down his face. Saw it spatter on the floor.

A man called out behind him.

"I know him! That's Frank Leslie!"

Footsteps behind him. Fat Ned Buntline was trotting along beside him.

"Frank? *Frank?*"

Lea paid no attention. Up above him, staring down from the great carpeted staircase, stood Sarah Bridge.

"Well?" Lea shouted up at her in his strange new voice. "Did you see? *Did you?*" She stared down at him as still, as white, as if she'd been carved for old Abe out of fine ivory.

He shouted up at her. "That . . . is *what I do!*"

He had said nothing more to her. He walked out to the stables, leaving blood behind him with every step. Toby Easterby walked with him and kept other people away. The Baron brought Edwards out to the stables afterward.

"I'm getting tired of patching you up, Mr. Lea."

Lea nodded. He was sitting on a stack of grain sacks while the doctor worked on him.

"This time I'm afraid I have some rather bad news for you."

"What is it," Lea muttered. His face hurt like hell.

Your opponent's bullet struck along the side of your face. Rather a bad wound. I'm afraid it's severed—or badly damaged—the trigeminal nerve. That means you will almost certainly have some permanent effect."

Lea didn't say anything.

"I think you'll have some paralysis on that side of

your face. At least a slight drooping of the side of the mouth. Perhaps of the eye on that side as well."

"My God," said Toby Easterby.

The Baron stumped over and patted Lea on the shoulder. "It will a good scar make, for certain."

"That," Dr. Edwards said, "is true enough." And he began to sew.

While he was working, Tiny Morgan came lumbering into the stable with Lea's bedroll and saddlebags.

"I got it all for you, Mr. Lea." He shook his big head sadly. It upset him to see Lea hurt.

"You are, by God, not thinking of traveling, Lea?" Edwards said.

"By God I *am,*" said Lea in that strange voice.

Edwards sighed. "Well, you *are* a fool," he said. "Hold your head still, and stop talking."

When he was finished, Edwards washed his hands in a basin of water. "Now, listen," he said. "Those stitches must come out in about ten days. And they *must* be taken out by a physician! There's some danger of tearing the nerve worse, if it isn't done very carefully. You understand?"

Lea nodded. It hurt a lot, just nodding.

Edwards dug into his bag, and took out a small, dark bottle. "Laudanum," he said. "You'll need it when that nerve recovers from the shock of the injury. One drop in a drink of water. And don't overdose. Bear the pain as long as you can."

Lea nodded again. He didn't want to hear his voice.

"Can we help you, old man?" Toby Easterby said, as Edwards was packing his bag. "I mean . . . well, there's no need for you to go!" The Baron nodded.

"Thanks," Lea said, in that thick voice. He got up

236

from the grain sacks to shake their hands. "But it's better for me to go." He forgot and tried to smile. It was like being hit across the face with a whip.

"You'd better take a drop of that laudanum, now," Edwards said.

"Yes," Lea said. "Thank you," he said to them again. "I have to go."

"But Sarah—" said Toby, and the Baron put a hand on his arm to stop him.

"I have to go," Lea said.

"Come," the Baron said to the others. "It's time we leave." He gestured to Tiny Morgan. "You come too."

"Good-bye, Mr. Lea," Tiny said. He was crying.

"Good-bye, Tiny," Lea said to him. "Remember those rainbows."

"We'll take good care of her for you, Lea," Toby Easterby said. "We'll see she's safe, and this business done properly."

Lea nodded, and lifted his hand, and they all walked out, Tiny Morgan last, looking back. He heard their footsteps on the cobbles.

Then he took the laudanum bottle, and scooped out a dipper of water from the water bucket, and measured a single drop into the dipper of water and drank it down. He rinsed the dipper out and hung it back on the nail. Then he put the laudanum into his saddlebag, and went back to the stall to get the old dun out and saddle him.

He got the old gelding saddled. Even that had been a job; maybe the laudanum had helped, and maybe it hadn't.

He was lashing on the bedroll when he heard her footsteps.

"Lea."

He turned to look at her in the dim lantern light, and she put her hand up to her face with a gasp. Then she came to him, and gently touched the bandage with her fingers.

"Don't go," she said.

"I've got to go," he said, in that slurred voice.

"Stay," she said. "Stay and rest. You don't have to see me. We'll *never* see each other. I promise. Just stay."

"No," he said.

"Please!" Her eyes widened. She leaned against him and put her arms around him. She held him as hard as she could. "I'll talk to Mr. Buntline," she said, her cheek against his chest. "He won't say anything."

"And the other people won't say anything either?" Lea said. "About me shooting that man to death in your hotel . . . in front of your guests." He shook his head. It hurt as much to do that, as it did to talk.

"Stay," she said.

He took her arms and forced her away from him, then turned back to the dun and finished tying the bedroll on.

"You don't love me," she said.

The Sharps was leaning against the stable wall. He went and got it, and slid it down into the rifle-bucket in front of the saddle. The dun looked better than he had for some time—rested, grained-up.

He led the horse out into the stableyard, and climbed into the saddle with a grunt of effort. The dun sidled a little, restless, rank from so much time in the stall.

Sarah came out of the stable, and reached up to hold his stirrup.

"Take care of the old Indian," Lea said to her. "Tocsen. Let him stay over the grain bin. He likes

238

it there."

"You don't love me," she said.

"Too damn much," he said. And he spurred the big horse forward so that she lost her grip on the leathers and almost fell. He trotted the dun out of the yard.

On a hill to the west, Lea reined the dun in, and turned to look back at Gunstock. In the distance, under a rising moon, the great hotel sparkled with a thousand lights—at the windows, the terraces along the ballrooms, the lanterns lit along the winding paths.

It was as beautiful as a dream. One of those dreams a man remembers and tries to dream again.

He looked for a while, then he turned the dun's head and rode away.